SWIPE WRIGHT

SWIPE WRIGHT

DATING IN THE AGE OF THE DISPOSABLE HEART

JOEL D. BRADLEY

Joel D. Bradley
Swipe Wright

Published by Ellis County Books
791 HWY 77 N, Suite 501 C
Waxahachie, TX 75165

www.elliscountybooks.com

Printed in the United States of America

Library of Congress Cataloging-in-Publication Data is on file at the
Library of Congress,
Washington, D.C.

ISBN: 979-8-9933651-0-7

DEDICATION

To all those adrift in the sea of lost connections—
those who have swiped right and been left,
who have stared at glowing screens hoping for warmth,
who have felt both the thrill of possibility
and the silence of disappearance.
This book is for the hopeful, the heartbroken,
and the hilariously human among us
still searching for something real
in a world that too often mistakes
motion for meaning.
May you find laughter in the absurdity,
courage in the chaos,
and a reminder that you are not alone
in navigating the strange tides of modern love.
—Joel

CONTENTS

CHAPTER 1

ALL GOOD THINGS

"When men are not needed, they do not become."

— **GEORGE GILDER,** ***SEXUAL SUICIDE***

The kiss of the rising sun lit up the dashboard of the first-generation Prius, ushering to life the majestic Golden Gate Bridge. Below the iconic span, the wind whipped the bay waters into a white-capped fury.

For Frank Wright, a deep, cleansing breath always brought calm at the start of his day. In the rearview mirror, he could still see his charming waterfront home in Sausalito, where his petite, pretty wife, Gail, remained nestled in bed alongside TC, their Maine Coon cat, fast asleep atop the covers.

Driving toward Golden Gate Park and Fire Station 11 had been Frank's routine for twenty years. Between his Styrofoam cup of wake-up coffee and the familiar voices on the radio, life felt comfortably habitual for the trim, forty-one-year-old Northern California native.

Frank exited the now-busy 101 and approached the park. He took in the beginnings of urban life stretching out like TC across the park's thousand-acre sprawl.

He lowered his window, inhaling the scent of budding flowers, and offered a small salute while passing the memorial commemorating the 1906 fire that had destroyed eighty percent of San Francisco.

Winding his way toward Station 11, he chuckled at the thought of his motley crew of firefighters—modern California in all its colorful complexity.

Oh crap, he thought. *I hope Roger and Jax saw my note about the Fire Chief coming this morning.*

As lieutenant, Frank stood out. Dark hair with grey at the temples swept left to right—more Northern California hip than regulation cut, a laid-back look that kept one foot in the present and one in the past. Sharp blue eyes stood out against the olive undertones of a face shaped by rugged Western European ancestry. Station 11's mix of ethnicities, new-age spiritualists, and self-proclaimed militants flew a flag of vibrant humanity. Yet his distinctly Irish quietude made him a cultural relic in progressive San Francisco.

He eased his Prius into his unofficial spot—a sliver of curb behind the station's side gate, just far enough from the red-painted hydrant to avoid a ticket, but close enough to shave thirty seconds off the walk. The space was shaded by a stubborn old sycamore whose roots had buckled the sidewalk into awkward waves. Stepping out, he slung his gear bag over one shoulder, the morning air carrying the briny mix of Bay fog and diesel exhaust.

"Frank! The captain called. Wants everything squared away before the brass shows up at 0800. That's eight ay-em for you non-military dweebs," shouted Jax Brown—Station 11's most decorated firefighter and former high school ROTC commander. He stood all 3'9" of authority, a micro-firefighter with a megaphone personality.

Roger, a towering former Oakland Raider with mountainous biceps and a worn NAACP shirt, leaned in as Frank passed.

"Hey Frank, Deputy Chief is on his way too," he added.

Frank picked up the pace, rushing past two female firefighters who were wrangling water hoses while *We Are Family* blared from the intercom.

Inside the north wing of the firehouse, a pungent odor stopped him cold.

He winced. "What is that smell? Jax! Get over here—now."

Jax hustled across the tile.

"Pretty sure it's Patty's fish, tofu, and cheese dip," he said, fanning his nose. "She's been workin' on it again."

"Ugh. We've got forty-five minutes to air this place out and prep for inspection," Frank groaned, already wiping sweat from his forehead.

From the common room came a protest.

"Hey! Turn that back on! They were about to share a new tofu recipe—for dogs!" Patty shouted.

"Patty," Jax called back, "Frank said all hands on deck! We're in some code color!"

"Well, what am I supposed to do, Jax?"

"I don't know—maybe clean the kitchen floor where everyone puked from the smell of your dip!"

The commotion swelled.

Frank's phone buzzed.

A text from Captain Gavin Newland—thirty-year veteran, part-Mormon, a trace of Portuguese from his mother, and a tireless braggart about both—flashed across the screen. His rise wasn't just time served; it was lineage. His father had been lieutenant governor under Jerry Brown back in the '70s, and the political scaffolding never came down. Newland was less a self-made man than a thirty-year construction project, built plank by plank through favors, optics, and connections.

Captain Newland: Heads up. Political brass arriving early. Look sharp.

Frank grabbed the station intercom, cutting off the Seventies Gold playlist.

"Code Blue!"

Crickets.

The team assumed he meant Old Blue, the station's beloved pug.

Moments later, Patty emerged from the kitchen with Old Blue dressed in a tuxedo.

"Hey Frank! Blue's ready for the Chief!"

"No, Patty! I said *Code Blue,* not *Old Blue*!"

Another buzz.

Ron.

Frank's best friend since his school days.

He ignored it.

Buzz.

Again.

"Dang it, Ron..."

A third buzz.

Frank gave in. "Ron, I don't have time. I'm trying to get the station ready for—"

"Frank, I'm in crisis, *amigo!*"

"What's going on, Ron?" Frank asked, watching two official fire department cars pull up.

"Depends, my friend."

"It depends on what, Ron? I've gotta go!"

"No, I wore Depends last night. The adult diapers. *Glorious.*"

Frank hung up.

As he turned to greet the incoming brass, one thought lingered.

How can Depends be a crisis and glorious at the same time?

"Good morning, Wright," said Fire Chief Reginald Jefferson, a heavy-framed man known for his PR finesse and scandal-ridden private life.

"Good morning, sir. Always a pleasure—"

"Wright, I'd like you to meet Mayor Eve Apple."

Frank extended his hand to a pale, striking woman with the grace of a fashion model—San Francisco's political poster child.

Before he could say more, Captain Newland rushed in from his beat-up Ford Ranger.

"Great. Looks like everyone's here."

Frank turned to summon the crew, but Jax appeared from behind Firetruck #13, stepping forward to greet the mayor.

To Frank's surprise, Mayor Apple bent down to embrace him, whispering, "You never called me back."

Jax smiled. "Nice seeing you again, Eve. Haven't caught you on the CB in a while."

Frank blinked, unsure if he'd missed an inside joke or just wandered into a conversation from another planet.

Frank motioned toward his crew, ready to begin introductions, but Captain Newland cut him off.

"Uh, Wright, don't worry about roll call right now. Chief Jefferson, the Mayor, and I need a word. Inside."

Frank's mental antenna twitched. Something was off.

He followed the top brass past the rigs and into the station, eyes narrowed. Inside his modest office—a 100-by-150-square-foot kingdom—framed awards blanketed the walls. Photos of Bay Area celebrities lined the shelf: a lifetime of service and civic pride neatly curated.

Chief Jefferson cleared his throat.

"Frank," he began, "we wanted to let you know how much we appreciate your service to San Francisco and the SFFD."

Frank stood at attention, brows furrowed, a puzzled look spreading slowly across his face. Two-day stubble hugged his jaw like soot after a slow fire—stubborn, uneven, and oddly fitting, though he knew the brass was arriving that day and had simply been too busy to notice he hadn't shaved.

Before the Chief could continue, Mayor Apple stepped forward.

"Lieutenant Wright," she began, "I wanted to personally come today and express the city's gratitude for your dedicated service to Greater San Francisco. As you know, we're in the midst of a transformative time—not just in Northern California, but across this Golden State. Change that demands bold moves and real leadership to chart a new path forward for all citizens."

Frank turned toward Captain Newland—and froze.

The captain stood silently, head bowed like a man attending his own funeral.

Frank's hand went up, palm open. "Is there something I need to know about, Mayor?"

"Yes, Frank," she said, smiling gently. "I'm announcing my candidacy for governor of California tomorrow. As you might know, the recent recall has made it necessary for me to bring my leadership to the people. California deserves steadiness in a moment of chaos, and I intend to provide it."

Frank blinked. *"Governor?"*

Before he could speak, Chief Jefferson cleared his throat.

That kind of throat-clear. The kind that came before a sucker punch.

"Frank," he said, "there's... another reason we're here."

Here it was.

The ambush.

The ceremonial pat on the back before the axe.

Mayor Apple placed a hand over her heart like she was about to sing the national anthem—or confess to murder.

"Lieutenant Wright," the mayor began, her tone measured, diplomatic. "With the city's new focus on equity, inclusion, and future-oriented leadership, we've had to make some tough staffing decisions."

Frank said nothing, his brow furrowing as the words settled in.

There was a pause. She offered a tight smile. "We're phasing out certain legacy roles as part of a departmental restructuring. It's not about you—it's about where we're headed."

He tilted his head. "So... am I being fired?"

She offered a practiced smile. "We're transitioning your position as part of a broader structural shift. It's not personal—it's policy."

Frank didn't flinch. "Eighteen years. Eighteen years of dragging people out of flaming buildings, patching up overdosed tech bros, and giving CPR to dogs in Patagonia sweaters—and now I'm being transitioned out? Or do you mean replaced for the sake of inclusive policy?"

A pause.

Chief Jefferson cleared his throat again, this time like a man savoring bad news he'd never lose a minute of sleep over.

"Well, replaced Lieutenant Wright."

"By whom?" Frank said sharply.

"Javier."

Frank squinted. "Javier who?"

"He, uh… doesn't technically have a last name," Mayor Apple said. "Or papers. But he's very passionate about fire. We found him living behind a Tesla Supercharger station in the Mission."

Before Frank could form a single syllable of response, a figure emerged from behind him—quite literally.

Javier stepped out from the shadow of a filing cabinet.

Where no one—*including physics*—seemed to recall he had ever been standing.

He was Frank's height and build, with dark hair and a warm complexion that could almost pass for Frank's after a week in the sun. His SFFD helmet was two sizes too large, perched atop his head like a birthday cake. "Hola," Javier said cheerfully.

Frank took a step back, visibly startled. "Where did he come from?"

"Oh, Javier is very resourceful," Chief Jefferson said, as if announcing a scholarship winner. "He's been shadowing you for the last two weeks."

Frank blinked. "Shadowing me? On calls?"

An uneasy Captain Newland chimed in. "Yeah. In my Ford. Right behind you on every run."

Frank's jaw tightened. "Two weeks? You had him tailing me like some bootleg surveillance op, and nobody thought to mention it?"

Newland gave a half-shrug. "Consider it... mentorship by proximity."

Frank stared. "Mentorship? You hid a guy in your truck like a stowaway in a cattle trailer."

Chief Jefferson nodded. "Shows initiative."

Frank slowly turned to Javier, who grinned and gave him two enthusiastic thumbs up. "You are muy brave, Señor Frank. I learn much from your hose technique."

Frank blinked. "Wait. What?"

Captain Newland cleared his throat but offered no help.

Frank looked back at Chief Jefferson. "Hold on... is he even —like—*on the payroll?*"

The Chief hesitated. "He's, uh... technically in a community engagement pipeline."

Frank's eyes widened. "He's not even legal, is he? Tell me he's not an illegal alien."

Mayor Apple leaned in, lowering her voice. "We don't say *illegal alien* anymore."

Smiling like she was cutting a ribbon at a charter school, she proclaimed with icy patience, "We prefer the term *Transnational Partner*." Her tone was the kind reserved for explaining recycling to a toddler. She let the silence hang, then added, "Because language shapes reality—and in this city, everyone contributes."

Frank blinked again. "You renamed illegal immigrants?"

"We're reframing the narrative," Apple said proudly. "And Javier here? He's part of a new visibility initiative. Representing voices that were previously... underserved."

Javier beamed. "Gracias, Señora Alcaldesa."

Frank ran a hand down his face. "Underserved, what is happening here?"

Frank stared at all of them, his mouth slightly agape.

"Javier's story is powerful," the mayor said, eyes gleaming with the kind of political passion usually reserved for ribbon-cuttings and fundraisers.

Chief Jefferson jumped in. "Crossed the border in the dead of night, thirty miles on foot, dodging rattlesnakes and choppers. Had nothing but a lighter, a dream, and a homemade chili recipe—used it to bribe his way past a rancher with a shotgun. Learned more about survival in those two days than most recruits do in a year. Brings a perspective on adversity in high-leverage situations you only get from outrunning border patrol through desert brush. That kind of grit can't be taught."

Frank studied Javier—it was a familiar face in a slightly off reflection. The skin was a shade darker, the hair parted the other way, the accent broken and uncertain.

For a split second, he didn't feel anger. He felt disoriented. Like the universe had mocked up a version of him, made a few edits, and hit "refresh."

Suddenly, it hit him: this wasn't a personnel decision.

It was a narrative.

Frank turned to Javier, who was now trying to extinguish a scented candle with his fingers.

"Yeah," Frank muttered. "He's ready."

"And because I'm a middle-aged white guy who actually knows how to put out fires," he added slowly, "I'm expendable?"

"You're not just a white guy," Chief Jefferson said. "You're a *cis* white guy. That's like... double-bad.

Frank exhaled through his nose. "Cis? What is that?"

The mayor chimed in, "It's a modern term for people who never change from who they are. California is changing, a resetting of traditional ideas and terms, Frank. Please understand that we are living in a..."

Frank interrupted. "So, after nearly two decades of risking my life, I'm being thanked with a heartfelt 'beat it' and a replacement who probably thinks a backdraft is a kind of movie."

The mayor nodded solemnly. "But we're giving you severance pay and a thank-you gift."

She handed him a green canvas tote bag with the city's seal. Frank glanced down at the slogan printed across the front:

Progress Never Rests.

He was pretty sure **the 'national razor'** was also what the guillotine operator told the aristocrats in 1793.

The contingent exited with the solemnity of a funeral procession for an old fire truck no longer in production. Chief Jefferson gave a half-hearted salute. Mayor Apple offered a firm handshake, her smile lacquered with political sheen and moral superiority.

Javier lingered a moment too long, waving enthusiastically at Frank like a tourist disembarking from a cruise ship.

Then—silence.

Frank stood alone in his office, surrounded by plaques no one cared about and photos of smiling faces that now looked smug with hindsight. He sank into his chair—his throne—and let the quiet wrap around him like smoke.

A few minutes passed.

Then the door creaked open.

Captain Newland stepped inside, shoulders slumped as if he'd just come from a dentist visit and jury duty on the same day. He closed the door and let out a long, defeated breath.

"Frank."

Frank didn't turn. "You left your spine out there, Captain. Thought you might need it."

Newland winced. "Look, I wanted to say something. I just... couldn't. Not with them there."

Frank turned in his chair, gaze hard. "So this isn't just about Javier's legendary love of putting out fires with his fingers."

Newland rubbed the back of his neck like he could scrub away the moment.

"The mayor's running on a new platform," he said. "Real progressive stuff. She wants to be the face of diversity, equity, inclusion... all of it. The new California model."

Frank stared at him, arms crossed. "And I'm what—collateral whiteness?"

Newland didn't laugh. "She thinks replacing you makes a

statement. Bold move. Fresh face. Preferably one that doesn't require a birth certificate."

Frank raised an eyebrow. "So that's what my pension got traded for—a campaign slogan?"

"I'm sorry, Frank. This wasn't my call. You're one of the best we've ever had. Hell, you trained half this station."

Frank let out a slow whistle. "Guess I should've learned to say *hose* in twelve languages and dodge my way through immigration checkpoints."

Newland chuckled—reluctantly. "I mean… it wouldn't have hurt."

There was a pause. A long one.

Then, more quietly, Newland added, "They asked me to be the face of the station moving forward. Media appearances. Social channels. Diversity dinners."

Frank gave him a long look. "*You?* Your mom's from Fresno."

"She's one-eighth Portuguese," Newland said. "From the Azores."

Frank leaned back, let out a single, sharp, joyless laugh.

"We're living in a cartoon."

Newland shrugged. "A very inclusive one."

CHAPTER 2
THE DISPOSABLES

"Every time we liberate a woman, we must be prepared to redefine man."

— MARGARET MEAD

The kiss of the rising sun lit up the dashboard of the first-generation Prius, ushering to life the majestic Golden Gate Bridge. Below the iconic span, the wind whipped the bay waters into a white-capped fury.

For Frank Wright, a deep, cleansing breath once meant purpose. Now it was more like coming up for air in a world that had quietly decided it didn't need him.

Instead of the scent of spring flowers on the way to Station 11, Frank inhaled the fumes of reheated burritos and the stale musk of male malpractice. He had become a cautionary tale in his own home—a ticking time bomb threatening his already frayed domestic peace.

In his new role as full-time unemployed husband, Frank's schedule had deteriorated into daytime reruns of *The Jerry Springer Show*, cereal in mixing bowls, and YouTube rabbit holes about "shapeshifting politicians." Gail—a neat freak with a zero-tolerance policy on chaos—observed his regression from a distance, her sighs long enough to register as psychological warfare.

To Gail, cleanliness was next to godliness.

Frank's new lifestyle didn't stand a chance.

Happy wife, happy life had always been a phrase Frank heard but never quite lived. Now he understood too late: happiness wasn't a stationary target. It was a moving, emotional bullseye he could never zero in on.

"Frank, I can't do this anymore. Not like this."

Gail stood in front of the TV console, her voice shaking—but not from volume. "On-screen, two women clawed at each other over a man named Rico, while the crowd thundered in unison—'Jerry! Jerry!'—a chant that sounded less like television and more like something primal."

Frank didn't flinch. He sat in his tattered robe on the sunken end of the couch, one foot in a faded argyle sock, the other in something orange and ghosted from Halloween. A crusted cereal bowl sagged beside him. Jerry mediated chaos. And TC, the Maine Coon, perched above it all—aloof and imperial, like a monarch trapped in a crumbling court.

Frank scratched his stomach. “Babe, it’s going to be fine. I’m just in between opportunities.”

“You’re in between episodes,” Gail shot back. Her arms crossed. Her whole body seemed folded.

Frank looked up at her. He could see the same—petite, pretty woman he had fallen for almost twenty years before. She was wrapped in natural light with an outline of a halo—but lately, the intimacy between them had evaporated. The air in the room felt heavy. He didn’t reach for her hand anymore. He reached for the remote.

“Frank,” she said, quieter now. “I need a partner. Not a roommate with a heartbeat. Not another TC.”

He glanced at the cat.

TC blinked. Judgmental. Smug.

“I’m trying,” Frank muttered.

“No. You’re existing. Barely.”

The laugh track from the television bled into the room, more mocking than amused. Gail winced.

“Frank, can you turn that off?”

He didn't. He thumbed the mute button instead, leaving the chaos playing out like a silent movie.

Gail didn't look at him—her eyes stayed on the flickering images in the corner.

"It's not just about the job," she said finally. "Or the dishes. Or the cereal in a mixing bowl." She shook her head, the words gaining weight as they left her. "It's... everything. You're not in this with me anymore. You're not even in your own life."

Frank closed his eyes, as if shutting out her face might make the words land softer.

"I don't know how to be anymore," he said, his voice low. "I feel lost. I mean, I used to run into burning buildings without thinking. Now I can't even—" He stopped, the rest caught somewhere between his chest and his throat.

She let the silence hang, her gaze steady. Two slow beats passed.

"Can't what?" she asked. "Wake up before eleven? Kiss me anymore?"

From the muted television, faces convulsed in laughter, a silent jeer that made the room feel smaller.

"This is difficult. I recognize we haven't been close lately. It's like my body knows I've failed. It gave up before I did. No rise. No fight. Nothing." The words were sharp but honest.

She didn't recoil. She just exhaled. Sat beside him—not touching, but closer than she'd been in weeks.

"Listen, I know this is a difficult time," she said. "But I'm tired of feeling invisible. You're like a ghost. And not the poetic kind—the kind that haunts people."

"I don't know how to fix it," Frank said.

"You don't need to fix everything. But you do need to show up."

He glanced over with a half-chuckle. "In my birthday suit?"

"Geez, Frank! I just need you to be present."

Frank nodded.

As the days grew longer, Frank remained cocooned in his inertia, unmoved by Gail's increasingly desperate pleas. His routine was calcified: cereal in mixing bowls, Springer reruns, and zero ambition.

After her early morning Pilates class, Gail returned home to find him in position—sweatpants, mismatched socks, eyes locked on the screen. Springer was refereeing a family implosion.

Gail stepped in front of the TV, arms crossed- again. "Frank."

He didn't look away from the big screen. "Babe, this one's wild. Jimmy Ray might be the father *and* the cousin."

"I don't want to hear it anymore." Her voice cracked like a whip. "It's been a month. No job applications. No laundry. You haven't even moved the basket."

He glanced around for backup. TC blinked from the windowsill. Useless.

"Well," Frank began, "I reached out to Jax. He said his cousin needs help in his promotion business—"

"Seriously?" she cut in. "You think promoting *midget wrestling* is going to put us back together?"

He tugged off one sock mid-toenail inspection and stood—barefoot, hair wild, dignity unraveling like a cheap tarp in the wind.

"First of all, it's not *midget wrestling*," he said. "It's *micro wrestling*. There's a difference."

Gail's arms flailed in frustration, the straw that broke the camel's back, shredded it, and burned the haystack for good measure.

"I'm giving you a reset," she said, voice trembling but clear. "You need to remember who you are without the helmet. Because I can't do this version of you anymore. I love you, Frank. But I miss the man I married. Get your stuff and leave."

He blinked. "You're kicking me out?"

"Let's not call it that," she replied, gesturing to the door.

"Since you're so careful with words… let's just say *inter-mission.*"

Ten minutes later, the door shut softly behind him. He stood on the doormat—WELCOME, the word now faded and cruel, as if the house itself was in on the joke. Through the front window, TC stretched with feline elegance, tail flicking with royal indifference as if to say,

I'll tell you how the paternity results turn out.

Frank shuffled toward his Prius, the pavement cold beneath his slippers, each step flopping against the concrete like applause for a show already over. In one hand, his car keys and phone; in the other, his departing tote bag stamped with the slogan *Progress Never Rests.* He glanced down at it—bulging with the ten-minute belongings he'd been allowed to salvage—then exhaled through his nose, sharp and humorless.

Yeah, he thought. *Neither does failure.*

His phone buzzed as soon as he sat down.

Ron.

"Frankie boy!" Ron's voice blared through the speaker. "Did you see that Springer ending? Gold!"

Frank leaned his head against the wheel. "Not the time, Ron."

"Perfect time! Springer *is* life, man!"

Frank sighed. "Goodbye, Ron."

“Wait! I got a guy—free cable. Doesn’t even need a ladder.”

Frank hung up.

Through the windshield, the hills rolled forward like a dare. His tote bag slumped in the passenger seat, deflated and metaphorical.

For the first time, Frank realized how far he had to climb.

CHAPTER 3
RON TO THE RESCUE

"...the life of man, solitary, poor, nasty, brutish, and short."

— **THOMAS HOBBES**, *LEVIATHAN* (1651)

The kiss of the rising sun lit up the dashboard of the first-generation Prius, ushering to life the majestic Golden Gate Bridge. Below the iconic span, the wind whipped the bay waters into a white-capped fury.

For Frank Wright, a deep, cleansing breath still brought a flicker of calm—but now it carried the scent of vape clouds and cheap detergent. In the rearview mirror, Sausalito had vanished.

Three weeks holed up in a Chinatown motel—with cold winds, colder takeout, and thoughts colder still—had stripped Frank down. With no place else to go, he called Ron.

Ron's loft above a vape shop in Oakland wasn't so much a home as it was a museum of mistakes. Motivational posters hung crooked. Autographed axes lined the mantel. Yoga influencers were known to drift through like pollen on a breeze.

Frank arrived with a single duffel and the look of a man who'd just walked out of a burning building—only to realize he lived there.

Ron handed him a chilled IPA—something aggressively named like *Hops of Anarchy*, all citrus bite and attitude. "This one'll either wake you up or punch you in the throat," he grinned. "Mi casa es tu bachelor pad. Room's down the hall —Farrah's waiting. I even cleared a drawer for your socks and regrets. Gotta run—mid-chat with a señorita."

Frank's "room" was a futon beneath a vintage Farrah Fawcett poster that fluttered in the breeze slipping through the broken top window. He sighed. Reclaiming his life wouldn't be easy. But it would be temporary.

As Frank sat down on the futon, he heard Ron shout from the living room.

"Amigo!"

Again: "*Amigo*, get in here!"

Frank wandered out to find Ron holding up his phone like Moses with a digital tablet.

"Behold—the pantheon of digital desire."

Ron, never married and a full-time enthusiast of online dating, was already plotting Frank's recovery through questionable swiping of virtual women.

"I just scored a two-week trial to **MeSoohoney.com**. This is going to be glorious."

Frank groaned. "How long have you been doing this? Five years? Seven? How many sites are you on?"

Ron didn't miss a beat. "**MixMatch, HoneyHive, YourOkimOk, LatinSeductress, JailBabes, EuroGams, RussiansNoDressing, LuvumandLeavem**." He tapped one more app with pride. "**Hearts.com**—this is where your journey begins."

Frank squinted at the pastel-colored logo like it was radioactive. He wasn't ready for this. He wasn't sure he'd ever be ready. He was still raw, still drifting in emotional debris, convinced this was just a test from heaven before some divine breakthrough.

But before he could argue—

"Did you see what Javier posted on Facelook today?" Ron asked.

Frank froze. "Javier? The job-stealing, *human fire extinguisher* Mayor Apple's using to stage her campaign?"

Ron nodded, deadpan. "Add 'wife thief' to the résumé."

Frank blinked. "Wait—*what*? You're friends with him on Facelook?!"

"Keep your friends close, and your undocumented fire-starter's closer."

He handed Frank the phone.

One glance.

And everything changed.

There she was—Gail—locked in what appeared to be a passionate kiss with Javier outside a taquería.

The betrayal hit Frank like a smoke grenade—no fire, just a thick, choking disorientation. The floor didn't drop out so much as shift, leaving him suddenly unbalanced in a world he no longer recognized.

That night, under dim lights and the dull thunk of steel meeting wood, Frank hurled axes beside Ron at a local throwing range. He hadn't said much for the first hour. Just threw, retrieved, repeated.

Ron squared up to the target, axe raised, eyes narrowing in concentration. As he was mid-throw, Frank blurted out, "Okay—show me the online ropes."

Ron turned his head toward him, grinning mid-swing, causing the axe to veer high, clanging off the brick wall and rebounding against the chain-link partition that separated the throwing stalls before coming to rest on the rubber surface below the target.

A staff member in a red "AXE-ELLENT SAFETY TEAM" shirt glanced over from behind the counter, eyebrows climbing, but said nothing. Ron gave a cheerful wave as if the wild throw were part of the show, then sauntered over to where Frank sat.

Now standing close enough for his shadow to fall across him, Ron hovered like a helicopter ready to lift off.

"My man. Welcome to the digital coliseum. The key to modern Cupid? The swipe. Speed matters. Don't read bios —scout the photos. Look for signs."

"Signs?" Frank asked.

"Yes, scouting signs," he said. "Think baseball—only more confusing signs… and fewer umpires."

He pulled up **Hearts.com**. A carousel of Bay Area women flicked across the screen as Ron swiped with ruthless rhythm.

"Too heavy—left. Too short—left. Cat lady—left. Ugly kids —left."

Frank blinked. "Ugly kids?"

"She's got two of 'em in the pic. Genetics don't lie, amigo. Bad DNA is a scouting report in diapers."

In under ninety seconds, Ron burned through thirty profiles. Then he froze—eyes wide, thumb hovering.

"Here we go. Your perfect Shakespeare match."

"Shakespeare?"

"Yeah—'If love be rough with you, be rough with love.' Or maybe the thumb-biting one. Whatever—look: raven hair, bikini pic, a little cross-eyed. That's why she posted the bikini—so no one's looking at the eyes. Swiping right."

He leaned back and drew a quick triangle on a cocktail napkin with the bar pen.

"See, Frankie, it's a pyramid. Attraction math. At the top? Bikini beats cross-eyes every time. Middle tier? No kids beats ugly kids. Bottom tier? Even ugly kids beat no sense of humor. It's survival of the hottest, the youngest, the least complicated. Women got their own pyramid. Just like us."

Frank stared at the napkin. "So what's below ugly kids?"

Ron grinned. "Simple. The sinkers. *'Partner in crime' bios, 'Live, Laugh, Love' quotes, or those lame dames holding wine glasses like they're auditioning for The Bachelorette.* Left swipe city."

Frank stared, hovering somewhere between horror and curiosity. "Are you swiping for me or you?"

"Don't worry about it. But, we need to build your profile," Ron said, cracking his knuckles like he was about to perform surgery.

Frank sighed. "Fine."

Later that night, alone in the cavern of his isolation, Frank registered to be a member of **Hearts.com**. He started with honesty—or his version of it.

First up: a high-res scan from a 1998 firefighter calendar, where he had been Mr. September. His hairline was heroic. His expression: accidentally smoldering.

Next: a wedding photo with Gail and his family. He rationed that family appeals to everyone.

For the bio, he typed and deleted. Typed. Deleted again. Finally, he settled on something bleakly efficient:

> Username: FiremanFrank11
> Profile Title: Looking for My Forever Flame 🔥
> Bio:
> Hi there! 😊 I'm Frank—just your average guy next door (if your door leads to a firehouse 🚒). I'm recently single and recently unemployed… but gainfully optimistic! 💪
> I enjoy long walks (bonus points if there's frozen yogurt at the end 🍦), grilling meat like it's a sacred ritual, and sunsets that make me feel like I'm in a romantic movie 🌅.
> Fun facts:
> I once rescued a poodle named Chairman Meow 🐩
> I still have a Hotmail account and check it daily 💻

> My favorite movie is *Backdraft* (don't worry, I'll explain why 😉)
> I believe in old-fashioned romance, handwritten notes, and mixtapes. Looking for someone adventurous, fun, and willing to teach me how to dance.
> No drama. Just maybe fireworks. 🎇

Frank leaned back, mildly proud of the effort. "There. That feels… honest."

He called out to Ron in the living room, expecting at least a nod of approval. Maybe even a *'not bad, Frankie boy.'*

Ron read it in silence, then winced as if he'd just watched someone hug a cactus. "Are you serious? Today's women don't want that crap. They want action. Beefcake, baby. They want a guy who fishes shirtless in JFK Wayfarers and flips tires for fun."

Frank squinted. "They want *what?*"

"A middle finger on the pulse," Ron said with complete confidence.

Frank raised an eyebrow. "That's not even a thing."

"Look at my profile." Ron pulled out his phone and scrolled through nine carefully curated identities.

"This one's me on a boat with three ladies," he said, proud as a peacock. "Women want to see you're already in the mix. Preselection psychology. It's primal—they're drawn to the guy who already has other women around. It screams 'worldly.' It screams 'alpha.' It screams Flavor Flav with a giant clock around your neck."

He paused. "Listen, amigo—women want flash. They want a guy who smells and looks like *I've arrived.*"

"I don't know," Frank muttered.

Ron kept swiping. "Here's another one—me at a black-tie charity for dying kids or something."

Frank squinted. "You're wearing a tuxedo jacket... with no shirt underneath."

Ron sighed, shaking his head. "Exactly. Shirtless with a cause. That's edgy empathy. It's how you win the room and the heart."

Frank gave a slow, reluctant nod—armed with exactly the wrong kind of advice.

Ron slid his phone into his pocket like a card shark hiding an ace. "Alright, enough about me. Let me see your profile again."

Frank hesitated, then handed over his phone.

Ron scrolled once... twice... then froze. His eyes went wide. "Oh no. No, no, no. Tell me this isn't what I think it is."

Frank leaned over. "What?"

Ron jabbed at the image. "This! Your *wedding photo*! In your dating profile!"

"It's a good picture," Frank said defensively.

Ron nearly dropped the phone. "A good picture? Rule number one of online dating: never post evidence you've already failed the job. Rule number two: don't make your future date wonder who the hell Gail is and why she's in a white dress. Rule number three—" He held up two fingers—"no kids, no pets, and no pictures where you look like you're at a hostage negotiation, which, by the way, is what a wedding basically is."

Frank blinked. "You're comparing marriage to a hostage situation?"

"I'm saying it looks like one," Ron said. "You're supposed to be selling mystery, not explaining why you're back on the market."

Within 48 hours, Frank's new profile included a picture of himself in Walgreens sunglasses holding a frozen fish above his head. His interests: fire safety, cats, early morning drives.

Username: *FrankTheTank2.0*
Profile Title: *Let's Make Questionable Decisions Together* 😎🐟
Bio:
Former firefighter. Current work-in-progress.
If you're into fire safety, cats that judge you, and early morning drives where I question all my life choices—let's talk.

One secondhand tux, a faded *Charlie's Angels* poster, and zero plants.
Powered by strong coffee, second chances, and silence during movies.
I once gave CPR to a Labradoodle in a Patagonia vest. Weirdly, not the strangest part of that day.
Looking for someone who laughs easy, forgives bad hair days, and won't flinch at a little smoke damage.
No drama. Not a philosopher, but I like a quiet morning of reflection, calling out gratitude to heaven.

The response was… disappointing.

Finally, after three days, he received his first message:

Dear Mr. Wright, I saw your profile and wanted to remind you that your dry cleaning's ready — Lupe.

Crushed, Frank turned to Ron, who was chatting with three women simultaneously.

"Hey," Ron said, "at least she remembers you."

But soon, the swiping took hold. There was something oddly hypnotic about it—each photo a portal to joy or chaos.

Later, Ron asked, "So… what kind of woman are you actually looking for?"

Frank almost said *Gail*—but he knew that would earn him a full can of mental wup-ass from Ron. Instead, he kept his eyes on the phone, the cobwebs of attraction stirring: half-forgotten memories, flickers of old longing.

And then, he asked the question that had haunted him all along:

What if love wasn't just a battlefield... but a broken algorithm in disguise?

CHAPTER 4

THE LONG AND WINDING ROAD

"You have unmade your bed, now you must lie about it."

— **JOHN HOLLANDER,**
SWAN AND SHADOW

The kiss of the rising sun lit up the dashboard of the first-generation Prius, ushering to life the majestic Golden Gate Bridge. Below the iconic span, the wind whipped the bay waters into a white-capped fury.

For Frank Wright, a deep cleansing breath felt less like calm and more like a reset button. In the rearview mirror, Sausalito had become a postcard from another life. Gail was no longer waiting. TC had defected. Now,

his mornings came with push notifications, profile bios, and strangers' faces blurred by hope.

Frank stood frozen outside Axe & Ale—Oakland's premier axe-throwing lounge. The irony wasn't lost on him: a recently separated man trying to revive his love life by stepping into a room full of airborne weapons, craft beer, and strangers who looked only slightly more stable than he felt. He sighed and stepped inside.

That morning, the emotional rug had been yanked out—again.

Ron, half-laughing over coffee, had read the post aloud:

> "WELCOME HOME, JAVI 🩶"

Geotagged from *Frank's own driveway.*

Gail had moved in the undocumented firehouse replacement. No marriage counseling. No phone call. No warning. Frank still didn't even know if Javier had a last name—let alone a key to his house. For all he knew, he was like Bono or Prince—just *Javier*. Feeling gutted, Frank dove headfirst into swiping—left, right, right, left—a blur of filters, cleavage, and bios littered with half-truths. Each swipe was a dopamine rush, and he was hooked.

In a moment of fragile hope, he matched with "Stefania"—an alluring woman in her mid-thirties with the mysterious air of a modern gypsy and the elegance of Eastern European roots. She described herself as a yoga instructor and numerologist, drawn to the invisible threads that bound energy, fate, and healing.

She spoke of wounded masculinity not with judgment, but with a kind of reverence, as though it were something sacred and worth saving. Ron said that she was hot and probably open to bad decisions.

Frank arrived thirty minutes early. Anxious. Sweaty. Underprepared. He ordered a shot of tequila and sat by the bar, watching a bachelorette party hurl axes similar to Valkyries in sundresses.

His phone buzzed. A text from Stefania:

Running 15' late. Sorry!

He ordered another shot.

From his view near the window overlooking the bay, a woman began approaching in slow motion—part sunlight, part silhouette.

And just like that, nineteen years dissolved.

Frank was twenty-two again, standing outside a flower shop in the Mission District, clutching a cheap bouquet and wondering if Gail would laugh at the baby's breath.

Now here he was again. Only this time, no flowers. No illusions. Just tequila, nerves, and a woman named Stefania who may or may not believe in the numerical value of houseplants.

She was taller than expected—and striking, in a way that sobered Frank slightly despite the buzz. Her shawl, sheer and fringed, shimmered with stitched half-moons that fluttered as she moved. A white tank and short skirt clung effortlessly, as if chosen without care but worn with instinctive grace.

Frank stood too quickly, knocking over a second shot glass. A tequila-soaked napkin clung to his elbow.

"Frank?" she asked, tilting her head. Her voice had a melodic cadence—unexpectedly soft, like a favorite song heard through a wall.

She smiled, eyes curious but unreadable. "Are you alright?" she said gently.

"Yes. Sorry—my foot was asleep. It's, uh... nice to meet you."

They sat at a high-top table just far enough from the chaos of the axe-throwers.

For the first few minutes, Stefania did most of the talking—her journey from Eastern Bloc conflicts to Northern California retreat colonies. Frank soon learned there wasn't much difference between the two worlds. Her recent certification in Tantra Reiki ushered a call for another shot of tequila from Frank.

Then came the inevitable question, delivered with a sultry lean:

"So... what brings you online for love, Frank?"

She said it with a tease—as if his answer might trigger a chakra or unzip the universe.

Frank reached for his courage, stalling. He wasn't about to say, *My wife left me for an undocumented firefighter who took my job.* That felt like oversharing... and losing.

"Just... trying something new," he said, shrugging with the grace of a man dodging emotional landmines.

Stefania's eyes narrowed, playful but probing. "Trying... or searching?"

Before he could respond, a cheer erupted from the axe lanes. A woman had nailed a bullseye and was now twerking.

Stefania clapped softly, serene and unimpressed. "I like it here," she said. "It's primal. Regressive in a healing way."

Frank nodded. "Yeah. Nothing says spiritual alignment like tequila and axes."

She smiled, the kind of smile that made him feel like he'd just cleared the first round of a very weird game show.

"So," she said, swirling her mezcal like a witch mixing a love potion, "what's your situation?"

Frank coughed mid-sip. "Oh, you know... temporary."

She tilted her glass, a sly smile tugging at her lips. "You mean a sublet?"

"More like... a spiritual dormitory," he said, then winced. "Didn't sound that weird in my head. I'm in transition. Healing era. Big changes."

Stefania's eyes lit up. "Good. I once lived in a yurt for six months after ditching a Scorpio who said he didn't believe in numerology. He even stole my tarot deck on the way out—probably to impress the next poor girl. At least he was consistent with his chart." She leaned in, her voice softening. "You're not a Scorpio, are you?"

She smiled, adding with a wink, "And you definitely don't strike me as a five."

Frank blinked. "That sentence had a lot of words I've never used before."

She laughed, draping an arm over the back of her chair. "Relationships are cosmic contracts, Frank. Every one of them teaches you something you didn't even know you needed to learn."

He nodded slowly. "Right. And what did, uh, Mr. Scorpio teach you?"

She closed her eyes for a beat. "That liars wear expensive cologne."

Frank chuckled. "That sounds... pungent."

"Oh, he was. I've dated tech millionaires, plumbers, even a guy who sold mushroom chocolate on TikTok. But none of them could meet me where I was emotionally. Mushroom chocolate—organic, ceremonial grade—opens your mind without wrecking your liver, in case you were wondering."

Frank stirred his straw and tried to mask the growing panic in his throat. If she couldn't handle a guy who sold mushrooms on TikTok, what would she make of an unemployed ex-firefighter crashing on a futon above a vape shop?

"Sounds like you've really run the dating gauntlet," he offered, trying to steer the spotlight elsewhere. "What do you think kept going wrong?"

Stefania looked up toward the ceiling, eyes distant. "Honestly? Most men are stuck on a spiritual first step. They mistake lust for love. Their egos are too loud to hear the soul."

Frank nodded, slowly. "Right. Loud egos. Ladders. Not ideal."

"What about you?" she asked. "What ended your last relationship?"

Frank hesitated. He thought about Gail and Javier's shared robe hanging in the master bathroom.

"We… grew apart," he said, keeping it vague. "Different priorities."

She seemed to accept this with a solemn nod. "It happens. Do you feel ready to connect again?"

Frank looked at her—soft eyes, celestial earrings, the faint smell of liquor and lime. He thought about the chaos he was avoiding back at Ron's. The futon. The existential dread between 2 and 4 a.m.

"I think I'm open to... possibilities."

She smiled. "That's all the universe needs."

They sat quietly for a moment, the sound of axes thudding against wood echoing through the background as primal punctuation marks.

The conversation had drifted into that stillness where anything more would feel like trying too hard. Stefania was tracing her finger around the rim of her glass, humming some song under her breath. Frank glanced at her, half-admiring the mystery, half-exhausted by it.

Maybe this wasn't so bad. He hadn't cried. He hadn't confessed. He hadn't mentioned Javier, the futon, or the hollowness of swiping through strangers as if he were shopping for emotional furniture. Maybe—just maybe—he could rejoin the world, a man among men, and not the punchline to somebody's dating horror story.

Then his phone buzzed.

He ignored it.

It buzzed again.

He casually turned it over on the table, but the preview banner lit up in bold font:

> Ron: Amigo, Javier just posted a video from your hot tub.

Frank froze. The words hit like a brick through a stained-glass window.

Stefania raised an eyebrow.

"Everything okay?"

He smiled, tight-lipped. "Yeah. Just, uh… my roommate. He likes to... post things."

Stefania nodded, half-believing, half-bored. "Social media is such a lower-vibration activity."

Frank chuckled, though it landed somewhere between a hiccup and a dry heave. Outwardly, he tried to play it cool, but inside his brain was conducting a full-blown emergency drill.

Hot tub?

Was TC in the video?

Had they used the last of the chlorine he bought before getting booted, not unlike an expired carton of milk?

Did Ron hit the like button?

Or was he too busy scouring the internet for a Wonder Woman poster to hang next to Farrah?

He blinked, then looked down at his drink. He needed something stronger.

Possibly holy water.

His phone buzzed again. This time, a photo preview popped up. There was Javier, shirtless, grinning with a cigar and two thumbs up, next to Gail—who appeared to be wearing Frank's old fire department t-shirt.

He stared at the phone a second longer before sliding it slowly back into his pocket like a live grenade.

Stefania tilted her head. "You sure everything's alright?"

Frank forced a grin. "Yep. Just remembered I forgot to take out the trash."

She raised an eyebrow, amused but unconvinced. "That's your way of saying the night's over?"

He hesitated, then let out a laugh that landed somewhere between a sigh and a groan. "No—just my way of saying I could really use an axe right now."

A few minutes later, they'd traded the high-top for an open lane at the far end of the range.

As Frank stepped up to the line, Stefania appeared beside him, balancing two shot glasses with neon limes jammed in the rims.

"To the full moon and new beginnings," she declared, clinking his glass.

Frank matched her enthusiasm a little too hard—the rim cracked against hers, and a splash of tequila jumped out, spattering her thin cotton top.

He winced. "Guess I'm more demolition than celebration."

Stefania gasped at the cold sting, then broke into laughter, holding the damp spot away from her skin. "Well, that's one way to make an entrance."

"I'm sorry!" he said, reaching for napkins that didn't exist.

Flustered, Frank threw back the rest of his shot, nearly choking as the liquor burned down his throat.

She waved him off, still laughing. "It's fine. I'm pretty sure this shirt's been through worse first dates."

A group at the next lane started filming—drawn to the strange little spectacle: a drenched numerologist in a moon-stitched shawl, a man with wild eyes gripping an axe like it owed him child support, and tequila shots flying like props in some unhinged séance.

Frank looked at the target, his face suddenly calm in that terrifying way that precedes either enlightenment or a public meltdown.

"Ready?" Stefania said, falling in beside him, adjusting her damp shirt and squinting at the target like she could hex it.

Frank didn't answer. He stepped up, drew back his arm, and let out a **primal scream** that echoed off the industrial walls like a wolf. The room went silent—axes paused mid-air, conversations froze, even the bartender looked up from rinsing glasses.

Then—**THWACK.**

The axe slammed into the bullseye, dead center.

For a beat, no one moved. Then someone started laughing. Then everyone did.

Applause broke out. Someone yelled, "Get that man another round!" Stefania clapped and bowed like a proud stage mom at a talent show. Frank turned, breath heaving, the camera phone crowd cheered. Somewhere in the digital ether, a video was already being trimmed and captioned:

> "Dude finds therapy through tequila and edged weapons. #BullseyeBreakdown#Axe and Ale #Beauty and the Screech."

And just like that, the stars had aligned- for better or worse. Frank just wasn't sure which.

CHAPTER 5
HOT TUB CONFESSIONS

> "Men weren't really the enemy – they were fewllow victims suffering from an outmoded masculine mystique that made them feel unnecessarily inadequate when there were no bears to kill."
>
> — BETTY FRIEDAN,
> *THE FEMININE MYSTIQUE*

The kiss of the rising sun lit up the dashboard of the first-generation Prius, ushering to life the majestic Golden Gate Bridge. Below the iconic span, the wind whipped the bay waters into a white-capped fury.

For Frank Wright, a deep, cleansing breath used to reset the system. Now it was just crowd control for his

stomach. In the rearview mirror, yesterday's life smirked at him: Gail in a hot tub with her new 'partner in progress,' and himself immortalized mid-scream, hurling an axe on an endless viral loop. What began in silence was now broadcast in pixels—and everyone had subtitles.

Ron was shirtless, wearing aviators and cargo shorts, sprawled across a second-hand white leather couch that looked as if it had survived divorces and a storage unit auctions. A cloud of lavender vape clung to the air—sweet, dense, and vaguely oppressive. The television was paused mid-meltdown on a reality show, a young couple frozen mid-yell in a foam pit.

Frank shuffled in from the back room, squinting through the haze, head pounding.

"You're famous," Ron said without looking up. "Well, not you exactly—your hot tub. Your ex. And the undocumented Don Juan she swapped you for."

"Oh, no. What are you talking about?"

Ron sat up, flicked his vape aside, and waved his phone like Exhibit A. "Three thousand likes and climbing. TikTok remix—Javier doing tub cannonballs in slow motion while Gail mouths a Luis Miguel love song. Top comment? 'GAIL UPGRADED. 🇲🇽🔥'"

Frank dropped into the beanbag next to the couch. "It just keeps getting better."

Ron nodded, deadpan. "And that's not even the kicker."

Frank raised an eyebrow.

"You also went viral, my man," Ron said, pulling up another clip. "The axe throw. That primal scream? It's a meme now. Caption says: 'REAL MEN SCREAM... AND STICK THE LANDING.'"

Frank groaned, burying his face in his hands. "I'm double-viral."

Ron grinned. "You're a two-platform disaster. But honestly? It's kind of working for you."

Silence. Just the hum of the fridge... and somewhere in the distance, a lone gunshot echoed through the Oakland morning.

Then Ron added, more quietly, "You good, man?"

Frank didn't answer; he just slumped deeper, staring blankly at the ceiling like it might offer a refund on the last 48 hours. Two videos—each viral in its own unfortunate way—spun through his brain. One captured him screaming in the vein of a wild man before landing a perfect axe throw. The other featured his wife and Javier soaking in *his* hot tub as though they'd just conquered Frank Wright and opened a bottle to celebrate.

Ron stood, stretched with a grunt, and strutted toward the kitchenette. He opened a cabinet stuffed with mismatched mugs, expired supplements, and something labeled *"horny goat elixir."* From the chaos, he pulled out a half-empty box of cereal and dumped it into a chipped bowl. Dry. No milk.

"You know what the real problem is?" he said, crunching between words. "It's not Javier. It's not even Gail."

Frank, attempting to massage the ache in his head that felt as though it had its own drumline, raised an eyebrow.

Ron continued, waving a piece of cereal in the manner of a TED Talk. "It's the Gilder Effect."

Frank squinted. "The what effect?"

"Gilder. George Gilder. Read him once during college. Anthropology genius, philosopher—dude was obsessed with the wiring of society. Wrote this book, *Sexual Suicide.* Said men are only valuable when they're needed. Historically, we built stuff. Hunted. Protected. Invented plumbing. Now? Society's got airbags, **Hearts.com**, and **Google Maps**. We're not essential anymore. We're accessories. Just throw pillows with back hair."

Frank groaned. "So, I went viral for proving I'm still primal?"

Ron grinned. "Exactly. You screamed, reminiscent of a caveman and hit a bullseye. That's the most useful thing any of us has done since college."

He popped another handful of cereal into his mouth, chewing as if he were a man throwing gravel into a well.

"You, me—we're relics, bro. Masculinity used to mean something. Now? We're just... background noise. Optional."

Frank, looking more lost than ever. "What are you talking about?"

Ron pointed with his spoon like a philosopher with poor table manners. "When men aren't needed to form homes, they become ornamental. Lost. Their energy turns to chaos—or worse, self-parody."

Frank frowned. "Self-parody?"

"Yeah, you know... James Bond. Late-stage Bond. Still slick, but mostly just cosplay. Maybe I post shirtless charity pics and hang out with yoga girls because deep down, I don't have a tribe. No purpose. Just vibes."

Frank let that sit. The only sound was Ron's spoon clinking against ceramic.

"Think about it. You've got guys who used to measure themselves by what they built—houses, families, even reputations," Ron said. "Now it's all measured in social media likes from strangers they'll never meet."

Frank shook his head. "That's pretty scary."

Ron smirked. "Think of it like fire. In the right hands, it cooks your dinner. In the wrong hands, it burns your house down. Same tool, different outcome. At the end of the day, it's nothing but a distraction from the emptiness underneath, *mi amigo.*"

They both fell quiet again.

Finally, Frank muttered, "Gail wore my firehouse t-shirt."

"Right. Women inherit your soul in pieces. You don't get 'em back. They wear them in the manner of trophies."

Frank leaned back.

"Hey, did throwing axes appeal to Stefania?" Ron asked, hopefully.

"I'm unsure," Frank said. "But she talked about mushroom chocolate and a Scorpio who stole her tarot deck."

Ron nodded slowly. "So… second date?"

Frank closed his eyes. "I have no idea."

"Hey, tell me about spilled tequila shots," Ron uttered like a teen boy as he held up his phone.

A brief but unmistakable frame: Stefania in a cotton tank top, straddling an axe lane with a drink in hand—and him, arms raised like some middle-aged gladiator, grinning, flexing firefighter biceps, and pouring shots on Stefania's now wet cotton tank.

"Who posted this?"

"Someone in the next lane. They hashtagged it *#Beauty and the Screech.* Classic! Now it's making the rounds. Man, you look like a freakin' legend!"

Frank groaned and dropped his bag. "Great. Internet immortality."

Ron smirked. "Nah, this is what you need. This is social capital, my man. Welcome to the New Virtual Order. You're a desirable male now."

Frank tilted his head and squinted his eyes.

Ron stood, animated, while redirecting back to his philosopher voice. "Don't you get it? Women don't want men who chase. They want men that other women want. Gilder called it. We're nothing but disposable tissues—utility males unless we can prove we've got options. In a world without marriage incentives, our value is only as good as our digital desirability."

Frank with an already too early in the day exhaustion look. "So what am I now? Clickbait?"

"No, bro. You're a brand. And that brand just soft-launched with a hot axe encounter, a smile, and a woman who could pass for a Bond girl."

Frank looked at the ceiling. "Kill me now."

Ron didn't flinch. "Not yet. Not until you monetize."

As Ron rambled, Frank's phone buzzed.

> Stefania: Had fun. Didn't know you had axe skills like that 😂. Hope your arm's okay. You throw like a retired lumberjack. 😘

Frank stared at the message.

The kiss emoji.

That had to mean something… right?

"Who is it?" Ron asked, already smirking.

Frank angled the screen away. "No one."

Ron pounced like a kid drunk on Fanta grape. "Oh, come on, don't lie. Was it her? Tell me she texted."

Frank cleared his throat. "She said I throw similar to a retired lumberjack."

Ron beamed. "That's affection. That's post-date sarcasm. That's a green light with neon arrows, bro."

But Frank didn't reply right away. He was torn between self-deprecation and trying to sound confident. The truth was, he didn't know the new rules. Was he supposed to wait? Respond immediately? Use emojis? Was punctuation too intense?

He typed, deleted, typed again.

> Frank (unsent): Had a great time too.
> You've got a killer aim. And a wicked smile.

Delete.

> Frank (unsent): My arm feels broken, but I
> will survive. Tequila helps, lol.

Send.

It was safe. Non-committal. Slightly charming if read in the right light.

Maybe.

Ron peeked. "That's... underwhelming."

Frank shrugged. "So am I."

The phone buzzed again.

> Stefania: That's okay. I'm into broken things.

Frank stared.

Ron leaned in again. "Dude. She just sent you a mixtape title."

Frank stood, suddenly restless. "I need air."

Ron pointed to the window. "Get some air. And when you're done, text her something with teeth. Remember, you win the jungle by swinging on vines."

Frank rolled his eyes. "What does that even mean?"

Still, he opened the window and took a breath of Oakland —half jasmine, half desperation.

Somewhere, as strange as it was, Frank thought that things might be looking up.

CHAPTER 6

STAR-CROSSED LOVERS

"In a world of dissolving bonds, relationships are easily entered and just as easily abandoned."

— **ZYGMUNT BAUMAN,** *LIQUID LOVE*

The kiss of the rising sun lit up the dashboard of the first-generation Prius, ushering to life the majestic Golden Gate Bridge. Below the iconic span, the wind whipped the bay waters into a white-capped fury.

For Frank Wright, a deep, cleansing breath still offered ritual—but it no longer guaranteed peace. In the rearview mirror wasn't just his old life, but a hundred new ones, filtered with algorithm gold: vegan stunt

doubles, mermaid entrepreneurs, pet cuddlers. Somewhere in that digital field of dreams was hope.

Being misunderstood wasn't the exception—it was the soundtrack of Stefania Tepes's American life. Her path began in Romania, drifted through Europe's bohemian enclaves, and crash-landed in the urban sprawl of the United States, where she finally found divination in San Francisco.

A restless soul with a majestic smile, Stefania's profile read like a tribute to her Enneagram devotion. She proudly listed herself as a Type 6 with a 5 wing, casting a wide net for like-minded seekers in search of security and depth. Her photos blended All-American girl-next-door energy with fortune-teller fashion, each one an alluring contradiction. And her digital calling card? A provocative line that walked the edge between whimsy and wisdom:

> "Let's reach for the stars—or at least remind each other we're made of them."

Was it a filter or a trapdoor? A dare to swipe right.

She listed her interests as:

- Somatic breathwork
- The pyramids
- Dark chocolate
- Occasional steak fries

- A loyal man who knows how to fix things

She had, once, tried deleting dating apps to find herself. But instead, she found herself on **Hearts.com** reading bios of men posing with sedated tigers or standing on boat decks in leopard thongs, holding fishlike totems of masculinity.

When Frank's profile had popped up—awkward smile, cheap sunglasses (*ughh*), no shirt (*double ughh*), hoisted fish (*strike three*)—but there was a single sentence:

> "Not a philosopher, but I love a quiet morning of reflection, calling out gratitude to heaven."

—she swiped right.

Now, fate had taken shape in the form of a viral axe-throwing video. Her phone wouldn't stop buzzing.

"Why did my roommate just send me a slow-mo video of us throwing axes and doing shots—with Nickelback blaring over it?" she asked, sipping cold brew from a mason jar in a park that smelled like eucalyptus and dog pee.

Frank shrugged, hands buried in his jacket pockets. "Same reason the internet exists—to haunt us forever."

"I look as if I got dressed during an earthquake."

He smirked. "Could be worse. You weren't screaming."

"Yeah, you screamed like a third grader denied dessert after that last throw."

They both laughed—nervously. The moment had the tone of a second date that wasn't quite sure it was one.

They sat on a bench beneath a tree that once whispered tunes during Haight-Ashbury's flower power days. Stefania looked at Frank, who had a small mustache from an earlier chocolate milk.

"It's funny," Stefania said, "how women are expected to showcase our 'depth' on profiles. Like, I need to lead with my astrology sign, love language, and preferred travel destination."

"And men?" Frank asked.

"Men need a dog, height, and some hint of purpose."

He chuckled. "I used to have a purpose before it kicked me in the gonads."

Stefania grimaced. "Ouch! What do you mean?"

"Ah, I'm just joking. Purpose doesn't always show well on a dating app."

Stefania narrowed her gaze. "Can I ask you something?"

She didn't wait for a yes.

"Do you think the rules of connection are different online than in person?"

Frank straightened up. "Completely. Online, I'm a seven who has to write as if I'm a ten just to get ghosted by someone who says they 'don't believe in tradition.' In person, at least I know if someone's weird right away."

Stefania laughed and added, "You're not a seven."

Frank looked surprised and was about to ask what she meant before Stefania continued, her Romanian accent softening the edges of her English. "But isn't all love kind of… a projection?" she said. "Online just speeds that up. People meet, project, and delete."

Frank became animated. "Yeah, but statistically, meeting in person has a better filter. You can smell someone's shampoo. That matters."

"Wow, Frank, you sound like a romantic. My friend once swiped left on this guy—said his profile picture made him look like he sold time-shares in Reno. Then she met him at a house party, didn't even recognize him, and now they're married."

Frank laughed. "Exactly. In real life, your lighting doesn't come from some staged photo shoot—it's the harsh glow of a fridge door at midnight. If someone still likes you after seeing *that*, it's true love."

Stefania sat back, adjusting the loose folds of a bohemian wrap that caught the late fall light.

"According to my buddy Ron, seventy percent of couples meet online now. Organic meetings are officially the minority. Basically, we're just playing in the Matrix—chasing dopamine loops."

She stared at Frank. "Geez, that's dark for an axe thrower." A small pause was followed by shared laughter.

Stefania's phone buzzed. Another meme. Another edit. This time, someone had cut the axe-throwing footage to Wagner's *Ride of the Valkyries*. She rolled her eyes and turned her phone off.

Frank's phone buzzed too, but not with memes. A text notification from the California Employment Development Department:

> `Your unemployment benefits are set to expire. Final payment issued.`

He stared at the screen as if it were a death notice.

Stefania noticed the change in his expression. "Everything okay?"

"Yeah," Frank lied. "Just... purpose kicking again."

She touched his arm gently, and for a moment, it was enough.

He placed the phone into his jacket pocket and forced a smile. He had six dollars in his checking account before the last payment. At least he had Ron to help him. Still, he was sitting next to a woman whose chakras were apparently aligned with his sense of humor.

Stefania, oblivious to his financial low blow, looked out

across the park where a woman was chasing a homeless person, begging him to take her five dollars.

"Do you ever think," she asked, "that we're all just pretending not to be lost?"

Frank blinked. "Like… right now?"

"I mean, generally. This whole thing—apps, vibes, curating your highest self. We're all just misplaced broken toys."

Frank weighed the imagery of broken. "You talk similar to someone who meditates and shops online at 3 a.m."

Stefania perked up.

"I do. A lot. Usually, while eating cake in bed. I used to date a man who ran a retreat center in Big Sur," she began.

"Of course you did."

"He called himself a masculine channeler. But he couldn't change a tire. He cried during sex and told me I reminded him of an ex-girlfriend."

Frank winced. "Sounds intense."

"It was. Then he started selling raw milk and moved to Wisconsin." She said, trailing off.

Frank was mildly amused, but inside, something twisted. He liked her. Genuinely. But his bank account was hemorrhaging, his manhood felt like it had been repossessed, and now he had to compete with a tantric crier who sold cow juice.

"Can I be honest?" he said.

Stefania looked at him. "I'd prefer that."

"I lost my job as a firefighter. My benefits are drying up. I'm not some axe-throwing dude who can smile his way through a recession. I mean, I believe in good vibrations, but sometimes the harmony from the universe sounds a lot like a Beach Boys song I would soon forget."

She didn't flinch. "Do you think I care about that?"

"Don't you?"

She paused, but not in the way that suggested judgment. More like a recalibration.

"I care about honesty. And being in the moment. The world's full of rich men who can't look you in the eye. Sounds as though you're in a bad place, Frank—but just listen to the unseen messages all around."

He nodded but had no clue what she meant about unseen messages.

"Still," she added with a smile, "if you end up sleeping in your car, I get shotgun."

They laughed. But behind the laughter were two people fumbling through a world that promised love with a swipe but delivered it with conditions. She wanted security, even though she mocked it. He wanted dignity, even as it slipped through his fingers.

"So, if I'm not a seven, what am I on the scale?"

Stefania smiled, radiant and calm. "Numbers may be in our DNA, but we're far more than a silly scale—especially one that may or may not reflect who we truly are at this point in the journey."

A gust of wind sent a napkin fluttering a few feet away, rising and spinning like it had somewhere to be. As they watched its brief, aimless dance, both sensed it—something larger was shifting. The gravity of new uncertainties pressed down around them, invisible but unmistakable.

CHAPTER 7

TOO MANY CHOICES

"We expect more from technology and less from each other."

— **SHERRY TURKLE,** *ALONE TOGETHER*

The kiss of the rising sun lit up the dashboard of the first-generation Prius, ushering to life the majestic Golden Gate Bridge. Below the iconic span, the wind whipped the bay waters into a white-capped fury.

For Frank Wright, a deep, cleansing breath had begun to feel mechanical—like a daily update he couldn't opt out of.

Frank had texted Stefania three times.

The first was honest:

> Frank: Had a great time. Any late-night shopping?

The second was hopeful:

> Frank: No pressure, but I'd love to see you again. I'll even scream less next date.

The third was desperate:

> Frank: Unless you died in a Himalayan crystal cave, a quick 'no thanks' would be appreciated.

She never responded.

Apparently, her chakras were only aligned with employed suitors.

Now Frank sat alone on Ron's beanbag, nursing a generic-brand seltzer and scrolling through **Hearts.com**, where his primal axe scream had apparently become an algorithmic jackpot.

His inbox was fatter than a squirrel eating out of a trash can in Texas.

Sharon, 44
Loveline: Big girl, bigger heart. And 40-yard-line Niners tickets.
Bio: I bring snacks to the stadium and know more about zone blitzes than your high school coach. I also do Reiki, but only for my cats. If you can't handle a size 18 woman yelling at Kyle Shanahan on Sundays, keep swiping.
Photos: Sharon in a Joe Montana jersey, flanked by nachos and what appeared to be a hairless Pomeranian.

Kendall, 51
Loveline: Private jets and climate guilt.
Bio: Former tech exec turned environmental lobbyist. I own carbon offsets the way some people own shoes. Let's talk glacier melt and masculine vulnerability while barefoot in Nepal. Tired of this whack-a-mole game. No conservatives, carnivores, or men who use plastic floss picks.
Photos: On stage at Davos, and another at a safari in Kenya.

Marlene, 59
Loveline: Medical actress. Three divorces, zero regrets.
Bio: I drink martinis for breakfast and once played bongos with Bono.
Photos: A steely gaze in a velvet pantsuit; another next to a broken statue of Aphrodite.

Destiny, 37 (sort of)

Loveline: Former bottle service goddess, now seeking spiritual redemption through tantric improv.

Bio: I've been sober for four months and celibate for three—unless you count eye contact. Seeking someone who knows his way around Napa Valley (I'm ready to fall off the wagon and into your arms). Bonus if you've ever been to Burning Man and cried.

Photos: Burning Man, body paint festival, feeding buffalo in Yellowstone.

Frank read them all, slack-jawed.

"Bro," Ron said from the kitchen, peeling back the wrapper on a 7-11 burrito, "you're officially male catnip."

"I just threw an axe and screamed."

"Exactly. Raw, masculine, unhinged—a rare digital treat for the ladies. The women can sense the chaos. They want it."

Frank exhaled and refreshed the page.

Thirty-seven new messages.

He clicked on Sharon again. Something about those nachos felt... comfortable. Or maybe he was just hungry.

Frank studied her profile a little longer. She wasn't his "type"—whatever that meant anymore—but something about her felt real. Maybe she wouldn't ghost him mid-sentence to go rebalance her moon water. And anyone who dropped "zone blitz" in a dating bio probably understood men better than half of San Francisco.

He clicked *Message.*

> **Frank:** Hey, Sharon. I'm more of a Cover-3 guy, but I respect your game. Would love to talk schemes and snack hierarchies. You free this weekend?

She responded within a minute.

> **Sharon:** Only if you don't mind a woman who yells at the screen louder than you throwing axes! Sunday. Levi's Stadium. My treat.

Frank blinked. "How did she..."

> ***Frank:*** *Wait... you mean, at the stadium?*

> **Sharon:** 40-yard line. Real seats. Real food. Real woman. Wear red and pray the Niners win because you might get lucky!

Sunday arrived faster than Frank expected. The afternoon was a crisp fall day when he showed up at Levi's Stadium in an old firehouse-issued red fleece, walking the line between ironic nostalgia and reluctant team spirit. Sharon had left his ticket at Will Call, where the line moved just slowly enough to cost him the kickoff. By the time he made it to her section, she was already on her feet, arms waving like a sideline coach trying to stop the clock.

Wearing a custom jersey that read **SHARON THE SHELTER**—a tribute, it seemed, to her twin talents for rescuing stray dogs and emotionally unstable men—she handed him a beer, some nachos, and a stadium program. A sticker on the front read: *You're already doing better than the last guy.*

"Okay, ground rules," Sharon said, eyes locked on the field. "I scream, I cry, I critique play-calling. Don't take it personally."

"Sounds like my marriage," Frank replied. "Minus the nachos."

She stared at him for a beat—deadpan—then burst out laughing.

As the game progressed, Sharon transformed. She called out linebacker alignments, dissected nickel packages, and screamed "Cover-2, you idiots!" with terrifying precision. At one point, she used a few chips and a rogue jalapeño to explain gap integrity.

Frank, stunned, actually forgot he was broke and had recently been ghosted.

"You sure you weren't a defensive coordinator in another life?" he asked.

"I was," she shot back. "Mainly under the covers, according to my ex-husband."

By halftime, Frank felt something unexpected: joy. There was no spiritual discourse, no Enneagram filters, no pressure. Just a woman who knew football, owned her body, and refused to let life bench her.

Later, as the crowd funneled toward the exits, Sharon turned to him.

"So, how'd I do?"

"Honestly? I haven't had that much fun in a while. I'm sorry the 49ers lost, though."

"You're vanilla but nice," she said with a laugh, "I crown thee Vanilla Nice."

She gave him a side-hug—strong, brief, and firm like a pulling guard—then lumbered toward the parking lot, unapologetically herself.

Frank stood for a moment, unsure of what had just happened.

Maybe she wasn't *the one.*

But she was *someone.*

And that, for a man with no job and too many unread messages, felt like a win.

His phone buzzed.

Ron:

HOW DID IT GO? DID SHE TACKLE YOU AFTER THAT LAST INTERCEPTION COST US THE GAME?

Frank ignored it.

Another buzz.

Ron:

BY THE WAY, I'M HEADED OUT TO LINE DANCE WITH A COWGIRL FROM FORT WORTH. YEEHAW!

Later that night, as Frank plopped down onto the beanbag chair, he began swiping fiendishly and randomly. Oblivious to everything around him, the front door creaked open. Ron strolled in, cowboy boots echoing, trailed by a beehive-blonde in fringe and rhinestones.

"Hey, amigo," Ron said with a grin. "This is Tammy Lynn. She's from Texas and knows how to wrestle steers and liberals."

Frank struggled with the chair, then gave up and offered his hand instead, meekly. As the Southern belle took it, he noticed a quick flash of ink on her forearm—"DQ," etched just beneath the skin.

"It's nice to meet you, Tammy Lynn. What's the DQ stand for?"

In a slow southern drawl, she smiled. "Dairy Queen, of course!"

Frank smiled. "Right. Sorry—don't know what I was thinking."

"It's alright, hun. I grew up in rural Texas, where Hunger Busters are life."

Before Frank could venture further down the dirt road of all things Texas, Ron jumped in.

"So… how was the game and your big love match?"

"She was great. Smart, hilarious, called out the defense better than Tony Romo. I think she scared the guy in front of us into rethinking his entire football worldview."

Ron leaned in, suddenly serious.

"...Did you sleep with her?"

Frank blinked. "What? No! We hugged. She patted me as if I were a third-string tight end with potential."

Tammy Lynn cut in. "Hey, hold on a minute! Be careful what you say about Tony Romas—they have the best ribs in Texas!"

Ron turned, blinking. "We were talking about Tony *Romo.*"

"Oh," Tammy Lynn said, unfazed. "Well. Him too."

Ron began scratching his chin. "Sounds… oddly nice, I suppose."

He barely paused before adding, "Do you want to see her again?"

Frank hesitated. "I don't know. I liked her. I just—"

He sighed. "I keep thinking about Stefania."

Ron shook his head. "Seriously? She's a poltergeist, amigo. Move on."

Frank tried to swipe out of his dating app with no success as he addressed Ron. "She was… different."

"Yeah, well, anyone not named Gail is different. You need someone who won't ghost you because Jupiter aligned with Mars."

Frank slumped a little deeper into the beanbag. "I don't know. Maybe this is all too soon."

Tammy Lynn, who had been quietly checking her nails, looked up. "Hun, this is none of my business, but maybe you oughta focus on you instead of tryin' to scam some girl at a football game."

Frank sat up, blinking. "What? No! I'm not trying—"

He stopped mid-defense as his phone buzzed—seven new messages. Ron and Tammy Lynn drifted toward the kitchen while Frank skimmed through them. Most were intense, unhinged, or featured filters with dog ears. He was halfway to despair when one profile made him pause.

Sheila.

A tour guide from Alcatraz. Killer bikini pic. Bio mentioned crime stories.

Frank typed out a quick message:

> EVER ESCAPE THE ISLAND, OR JUST WATCH OTHERS TRY?

Without waiting for a reply, he dove back into the digital sea like a man late for a train.

Left.

Left.

Maybe.

Strong possibility.

Whoa—former NFL cheerleader?

Swipe right. Fast.

By the time Ron returned with a paper plate stacked with nachos, Frank looked as though he was defusing a bomb made of dating profiles—tapping, swiping, second-guessing.

Tammy Lynn two-stepped after him, patting her beehive like it was a Fabergé egg.

"Listen, sugar," she said, leaning over to Ron. "If you're chasin' a Texas gal, you better put jalapeños on everything—*even your cereal.* And get an air fryer. Down there, even the air's fried."

"Copy that," Ron replied, saluting with a nacho.

She nodded solemnly and resumed teasing her hair with a pink pen.

Frank kept swiping in the manner of a man sanding a memory down to dust. Ron looked over, saw the trance-like scrolling, and shook his head.

"Hey, amigo," he said, "are you okay?"

Frank didn't look up. "She'll text. Eventually. Maybe something came up—work stuff… lunar eclipse? Venus throwing a tantrum?"

Ron sighed. "Frank, you're not waiting for Stefania. You're waiting for a notification that isn't coming. She bailed like an Airbnb renter—checked out early and didn't even take the free shampoo."

Frank stared at his screen. "She said she would live in the front seat of my car."

Ron grabbed the remote, cheese dripping from his chin. "Amigo."

Frank wobbled before standing up, phone still clutched in his hand. "I'm going for a walk."

Ron didn't miss a beat. "Bring your phone. Just in case she doesn't text again."

Tammy Lynn called after him, still patting her hive. "And wear boots! Ain't nothin' worse than heartbreak and loafers!"

Feeling a sudden impulse of compassion, Tammy Lynn caught up to Frank, and with a voice soft but firm.

"I'm sorry, sweetpea—sometimes silence *is* the message."

CHAPTER 8

FORTUNE COOKIE

"About a third of my cases are not suffering from any clinically definable neurosis, but from the senselessness and emptiness of their lives... They are neurotics in the sense that they are cut off from the roots of their being, and they are defenseless against the diseases of the mind."

— **CARL G. JUNG,** *MODERN MAN IN SEARCH OF A SOUL* (1933)

The kiss of the rising sun lit up the dashboard of the first-generation Prius, ushering to life the majestic Golden Gate Bridge. Below the iconic span, the wind whipped the bay waters into a white-capped fury.

For Frank Wright, a deep, cleansing breath had become less about calm and more about bracing for impact. The profiles blurred. The names changed.

On the second call, she sent him a Christmas photo—Sheila and her sister in front of a fireplace, matching sweaters, mugs in hand, smiles wide and easy. Both were attractive, though Sheila stood out.

Her sister was the remix version—same face, just a little heavier.

Frank stared a little too long, then felt guilty—and also, unavoidably, curious. If things didn't pan out with Sheila... would that be wrong?

Absolutely.

Still, comforting to know the bench was deep.

Conversations stayed easy. Sheila had two rescue cats named Purrlock Holmes and Clawdia. She claimed windsurfing kept her "less stabby." Frank confessed he hadn't tried the waves since high school, and even then, he mostly resembled a flag caught in a rip current.

By the third call, something clicked. Not fireworks—more like the steady pilot light on a stubborn stove. Reliable. Kind of warm.

"You know," Sheila said, "I haven't met anyone who loves cats and has seen *A Few Good Men* more than five times."

Frank grinned. "You can't handle…how accurate that is." He laughed, misquoting the movie.

They made plans to meet in Chinatown. Neutral ground. Tea, noodles, window seat. No big expectations.

When Frank told Ron, the reaction was immediate.

"Chinatown?" Ron said, grinning. "Solid play. If it bombs, just grab some dumplings on the way out. Nobody looks heartbroken carrying a box of dumplings."

Frank cracked a smile—the real kind.

"Yeah. This one feels… less like chasing shadows," he laughed.

He arrived at the Golden Duck ten minutes early and spent nine of them convincing himself to stay.

Then Sheila walked in.

It took him a moment to recognize her. She was not the woman from the Alcatraz bikini photo. Or the Christmas picture. Or anything taken after the invention of the iPhone.

She scanned the room as if she was already disappointed and made a beeline for Frank, who stood awkwardly, half-smiling.

"Sheila?"

"Well, I'm always late," she said. "So—I get bonus points for consistency."

She sat without waiting, hanging her purse on the back of the chair as though it might attack her.

Frank took his seat. Her perfume arrived three seconds after she did. It was loud, powdery, and had hints of bitterness and mothballs.

Within minutes, the waiter approached. He never stood a chance.

"Is the tea organic?" Sheila asked, one brow already raised. "And not the cheap kind. I don't want leaves that taste as though they were stepped on in a warehouse in Fresno."

The waiter blinked.

"And is your soy sauce low-sodium or just low effort?" Sheila asked, eyes narrowing at the menu.

Frank tried a polite smile, but Sheila was already rolling.

She launched into a monologue about her job—how tourists didn't tip, how they asked dumb questions, how one once tried to vape inside a solitary confinement cell.

Then came the rant about dating apps.

"Everyone lies," she said, stabbing at the air with her chopsticks. "I mean, who is actually thirty-eight with abs? Filters, angles, lighting tricks—nothing's real anymore."

Frank sipped his tea, stealing a glance across the table.

She didn't catch the irony. She was too busy criticizing the spring roll for "being too hard."

It was hard not to stop replaying that Christmas photo—the one she'd texted during their second call. Two women in matching sweaters, framed by soft light and a roaring fireplace. Back then, Frank had assumed Sheila was the one on the left. The slimmer one. The one who later popped up in the Alcatraz bikini shot.

Now, under the cold glare of Chinatown's overhead fluorescents, he realized he'd been wrong.

Painfully wrong.

The woman in the bikini photo was Sheila's sister. The woman across from him was Sheila—same face, just padded in places the photo hadn't disclosed, her features softened like a painting left out in the rain.

Frank cleared his throat, trying to line up the memory with the reality.

"So, just to clarify… in that Christmas picture—was that your best friend?"

Sheila shook her head, steady with her tea.

"My sister. Celeste. Why?"

"Well. She just looked… I don't know." His voice drifted off, searching for safe ground.

"She's a phony," Sheila said. "Had work done. Fillers, filters, the whole package. You think she looks like that in real life? Please."

Frank nodded, forcing a smile.

"Yeah. Honesty's... rare."

Frank glanced at the door.

He wondered how fast he'd have to run to disappear into a Chinatown alley without drawing attention. Maybe Ron had been right. He should've picked the fortune cookie factory—easy to vanish, and the rejection would come with a proverb.

Trying to salvage the moment, Frank launched into a mid-tier story about cats.

"So I told TC, 'You handle the rodents, I'll handle the mortgage,' and my cat just looked at me as if I'd just overdrafted his Fancy Feast account."

Sheila blinked. Then she shifted to one side slightly.

A sharp release of gas cut the air—halting, offensive.

The kind of sound that stops all conversation, even in neighboring time zones.

The waiter, mid-pour with the water pitcher, winced like he'd stepped on a nail.

Frank, ever polite, pretended not to notice. So did Sheila, though her nose twitched, as if trying to confirm whether it had actually happened.

"Sodium bastards," she muttered. Then, suddenly, "Excuse me." She grabbed her purse, not unlike a parachute and headed off toward the restroom, one black sandal slapping unevenly against the tile.

Frank stared at the Golden Gate mural across the room, then down at the table—two half-eaten dumplings, a mangled spring roll, and a strong sense of delusion.

He raised his hand for the check. The waiter was already there, sliding it over like a hostage note.

Frank handed over his credit card without a word.

Declined. Forced to use his debit card, he prayed there was enough to cover the $32.57.

Success.

He was pushing his chair back—freedom within reach—when Sheila returned.

Trailing behind her, clinging defiantly to her sandal, was a pale white ribbon of toilet tissue.

Frank saw it.

The waiter saw it.

A nearby toddler saw it and pointed.

Sheila didn't.

She sat back down with the confidence of someone who had never once doubted herself.

"Anyway," she said, brushing hair from her face, "thanks for dinner. You're sweet, but this isn't a match. I've had more fun throwing rocks off Alcatraz."

Frank nodded, numb.

"Well… at least the rocks don't have gas."

She didn't respond—too busy wrestling her purse onto her shoulder. Without another word, she stood and walked out, the papery flag still trailing behind her, flapping just enough to feel like a warning sign for the next poor soul.

Frank sat frozen, half-wondering if he should salute it—or just the fact that she'd managed to ghost him in broad daylight.

He sat for a moment longer, alone at the table, surrounded by the scent of lingering soy and regret.

Shaking his head slowly, he looked down at his phone.

The glow of the dating app icon stared back like an old wound.

He swiped. Once.

Then again.

CHAPTER 9
BITING THE APPLE

"One is not born, but rather becomes, a woman."

— **SIMONE DE BEAUVOIR,**
THE SECOND SEX

The kiss of the rising sun lit up the dashboard of the first-generation Prius, ushering to life the majestic Golden Gate Bridge. Below the iconic span, the wind whipped the bay waters into a white-capped fury.

For Frank Wright, a deep, cleansing breath did little to cut through the fog inside. Somewhere along the line, decisions had been made—quietly, confidently—and he hadn't been in the room for any of them. He'd been voted off the island. No speech. No torch. Just gone.

As the sun dipped behind Eureka and Noe Peaks, the sky unfurled into a canvas of gold and violet brushstrokes. A cool coastal breeze swept through, gliding over the skyline with the grace of an artist's hand. The scent of jasmine—as if plucked from Nebuchadnezzar's hanging gardens—perfumed the fall evening air.

The Twin Peaks towered in silhouette, framing the rooftop garden of Mayor Eve Apple's mansion—perched high in the Marin Headlands, far from the Mission District, yet close enough to claim cultural proximity when politically convenient. The estate itself loomed with cinematic splendor and menace: solar-powered, with an infinity pool spilling into the horizon, and monitored by more drones than a militarized border. Below, San Francisco settled into twilight, its streets dotted with headlights and office windows, the fog drifting in without urgency.

Javier had never tasted caviar before. The salty pearls burst on his tongue, delicate and strange—nothing like a tortilla chip, but his mind instinctively searched for the familiar and for border agents. For a fleeting moment, he reflected on his odyssey from the cartel-shadowed jungles of Honduras to the polished plateaus of American high society.

Gail, meanwhile, was adapting with little thought to her eighteen-year marriage to Frank, whose repeated attempts to reconcile with her stopped after photos of Javier watching television with TC appeared on social media. New chapters were being written with modern updates—even her yoga pants had graduated from Target to Lululemon. Her smoothie ingredients now included kelp and spirulina —because in Gail's new world, the greener the sludge, the higher the virtue.

A small fleet of young interns now managed her *Wellness for Bay Women* podcast, a project Mayor Apple had graciously "curated" into the public spotlight as part of her new messaging campaign for women.

Beneath a glass pergola strung with soft, eco-friendly lights, the murmur of conversation mixed with the clink of glasses. Javier stood tall in an open-collared linen shirt, sipping Maison Perrier as he posed between a trans-rights activist and a biotech CEO turned vegan Buddhist. His expression —part humble, part bewildered—had become the unofficial face of Mayor Apple's gubernatorial push: Empathy, Equity, and Electric Scooters—3E for short.

Gail stood nearby, polished and poised, sipping Napa Valley chardonnay. She wore a designer knockoff cocktail dress and a freshly minted persona—one crafted by Eve's media team: *Domestic Strategist*. A reformed homemaker for the 21st century. No longer a relic from America's patriarchal past, she was walking hand-in-hand with progress—at least until the election.

But behind the retouched foundation and rehearsed gratitude stood a woman in quiet conflict. Gail had spent a lifetime mastering the art of control. And now, she was being told to let go—publicly, proudly, and on camera.

Born in Kansas, raised in a God-fearing, flag-waving farmhouse, Gail had once embodied the "heartland sweetheart." Her parents taught hard work, prayer before dinner, and the necessity of a strong man to hold the roof up when the wind came. She was supposed to be the first member of her family to have graduated from college—much less Stanford University—where she had been offered a full scholarship to study environmental engineering.

Hers would be a future rooted in science, structure, and solving real problems.

But she gave it all up after falling for Frank during her freshman year, while attending a CPR certification class he was conducting.

They made a good team—if good meant safe. Gail poured everything she had into their Sausalito home: recipes passed down from Midwest cookbooks, pristine white towels folded into thirds, and Pinterest holiday décor that matched the seasons like clockwork.

Children never came.

Doctors called it unexplained. She called it God's mystery.

So, she doubled down on her domain, finding purpose in being indispensable to Frank while pushing back the progressive tenor of modern women in Northern California.

But then came the earthquake—Frank's job was gone, swept out from under him in the city's sudden need for performative equity. And in his place came Javier; however unorthodox, the moment commanded it.

Javier, with his perfect posture, crooked smile, and kind demeanor. Javier, who arrived from Honduras by way of a 5,000-person caravan. He was riding San Francisco cable cars during the day and sleeping on someone's cousin's roof at night, before somehow walking straight into Station 11 like it was destiny. He was everything Frank wasn't anymore: energized, exotic, employable.

But what caught Gail off guard wasn't the differences—it was the eerie resemblance. Same quiet strength in the shoulders, same steady gaze, even hints of a cowlick that refused to stay down.

When she first met Javier at an outdoor barbecue hosted by Jax, she did a double-take. From a distance, for a flicker of a second, she thought it was Frank. A younger, sun-kissed version with less wear in the eyes and more ease in the smile.

She hadn't meant for the conversation to last. Her high school Spanish—four years of verb charts and Taco Bell orders in Manhattan, Kansas—hadn't prepared her for much. But Javier was simple in the best way: kind without being soft, attentive without trying. He reminded her of Frank, before the silence, the sighs, and the midday *Jerry Springer* marathons.

Maybe it was the wine—three glasses of Chardonnay and a

flicker of something she hadn't felt in years—but when Javier leaned in and kissed her, she didn't pull away.

Gail hadn't planned for her marriage to spontaneously combust either, but that's how lint fires worked—years of emotional buildup, too small to notice until suddenly it wasn't. One careless spark.

Poof.

Frank was out.

And Javier?

Javier was holding the hose.

Now, at Eve's fundraiser, she stood beside him like they were soulmates from a Sundance documentary—as if their courtship had depth, their story had pages, and this new life wasn't just a costume stitched together by consultants. But in a world where you can identify as anything that feels true, why not believe the fantasy?

Especially when it comes with kombucha, catered applause, and a guesthouse bigger than her childhood home.

But behind the retouched foundation and rehearsed gratitude stood a woman in quiet conflict...

... and she wasn't the only one.

Mayor Eve Apple, framed by ivy walls and candlelight, looked the part of San Francisco royalty—but she hadn't always walked red carpets. She had been manufactured, in the same way as many politicians, in the incubator of legal lights. Born to progressive attorneys in the redwood-fringed hills of Marin County, her parents had marched with Angela Davis and litigated against Reagan-era zoning codes. From Stanford undergrad to Stanford Law, Eve was top of her class—top of every room, really—and climbed the political ladder with the cool precision of someone who knew which rungs were greased and which were gilded.

She clerked, practiced, and prosecuted. But politics didn't find her until the lobbyists did—power brokers who understood that a brilliant, beautiful woman who could cry on cue and filibuster in heels was more valuable than any campaign slogan. Eve didn't just get elected—she was drafted into relevance.

But beneath the designer hemp wardrobe and surgically controlled optics lived a woman with eccentric tastes.

Truckstops.

Specifically, truckers.

It began during law school—nights of insomnia and invisible stress. One midnight detour off I-5 led her to a truck-stop diner where she sat in anonymity, sipping burnt coffee and talking axle ratios with a man who called her "darlin'" without irony. There, she found something oddly honest in the grease, the gear shifts, and the gravelly voices. Men who didn't know or care that she could quote the Ninth Circuit's dissenting opinions by memory.

She returned often, anonymously—no makeup, hair tucked under a cap, thermal shirt, and old jeans. The truckers started calling her a **mudflapper**, a nickname for women who lingered near the rigs—half groupie, half mystery. Eve never corrected them. She liked how it sounded—earthy, low-class, undeservedly sexy.

Of course, no one in the Bay Area knew. Her team would've seized up like a Zoom call on hotel Wi-Fi at the thought.

But Eve still kept the cap.

Eat Sleep Haul Repeat it read, tucked discreetly beneath her bed, a relic from a past no voter would believe.

From the podium, Mayor Eve Apple raised her arms like a revivalist preacher. "Tonight, we stand with the dream of a California that reflects the faces of its people. Not just the powerful—but the possible."

The crowd erupted in applause. Cameras flashed. Javier nodded graciously.

And somewhere in a vape-fogged loft under the watchful eyes of Farrah Fawcett, Frank Wright stared at the livestream, whispering to himself, "I used to be the possible."

From behind a melting ice sculpture podium—carved by a gender-fluid performance artist flown in from Reykjavík—

Mayor Eve Apple delivered her remarks with the urgency of someone whose principles were dripping onto a reclaimed hardwood floor…

CHAPTER 10

PLAYING WITH FIRE

"Those who have a 'why' to live, can bear with almost any 'how.'"

— **VIKTOR E. FRANKL,**
MAN'S SEARCH FOR MEANING

The kiss of the rising sun lit up the dashboard of the first-generation Prius, ushering to life the majestic Golden Gate Bridge. Below the iconic span, the wind whipped the bay waters into a white-capped fury.

For Frank Wright, a deep, cleansing breath still offered routine, but routine didn't mean readiness. These days, fire came in different forms. It wore lipstick. Asked questions.

Frank didn't mean to have two jobs—it just kind of happened.

The first came from Captain Newland. Or as Frank called him, Clipboard Barney.

Technically, it was a favor. A part-time gig teaching city-mandated fire safety classes at the community center: *Stop, Drop, and Roll Over*. Newland had pitched it like a lifeline.

"Frank, you've got two decades of experience and half a pension—why not stay and use your knowledge until this political wave ends, or at least use it to surf?"

What he didn't mention was that the gig came with PowerPoint slides, folding chairs from the 1960s, CPR dummies that smelled like flip-flops, and more liability forms than fire extinguishers.

Frank hated every minute of it.

The students were either glazed-over Gen Z interns sentenced by HR or anxious homeowners obsessed with sprinkler systems and YouTube fireproofing hacks. Last week, a guy named Bryce raised his hand and asked if his Himalayan salt lamp was considered an "open flame."

Frank told him only if it started chanting.

The second job—Uber—was an act of desperation wrapped in denial. He told himself it was just a way to "stay active."

Truth was, Frank needed the cash. And something—

anything—that made him feel like he was still moving forward.

He drove mostly at night. Riders blurred together—nihilistic tech bros preaching the end of capitalism, polyamorous art teachers sketching theories in the backseat. One couple nearly broke up over whether their dog needed gluten-free kibble. He didn't judge. He just kept the AC on and the radio low.

The contrast between his two jobs amused him in a dark way: by day, a pretend authority figure in a polyester polo; by night, a glorified chauffeur rated by strangers on their phones. At times, after his fire safety class, Frank felt like Clark Kent ducking into a phone booth—only to emerge as a burned-out Superman with no cape, no powers, and a two-star Uber rating. One job praised his experience and ignored his soul. The other didn't care who he was—as long as the ride was smooth and the auxiliary cord worked.

Frank didn't mind the quiet of riding at night. When the streets emptied and the city buzzed beneath the glow of streetlamps, he could forget—Stefania, Gail, Javier, the pension fading out of reach. For a few blocks, he was just a man in motion, far removed from purpose. Even dating was a form of psychological autopilot, unsure if he was searching for love or just proof he still had a pulse of value.

Another 9 a.m. fire safety class. Frank could practically deliver the presentation in his sleep—and some days, he did, eyes open. He knew the exact moment he lost the room: right between *Class K extinguishers* and the ignition point of canola oil. That's when the glazed eyes set in, and people mentally wandered off to their lunch plans.

Not Nancy.

She sat in the second row of the community center's multi-purpose room, notebook open, pen moving—not doodling, actually writing. No eye rolls, no sighs, no glancing at her phone like it was oxygen.

She raised her hand halfway through the segment on kitchen fires.

"Question," she said. "Do fire extinguishers expire? Because my old one looked like it came with the house... in 1987."

Frank blinked. Most people asked about pets or microwaves, or where the bathrooms were located.

"Yes," he said, surprised by how normal it felt to give an answer that wasn't dripping with sarcasm. "Extinguishers have a lifespan—usually 10 to 12 years. You should check the pressure gauge. If it's in the red—"

"I tossed it a while back," she said. "The only thing good from 1987 is an old Duran Duran video."

He laughed.

She smiled. "I lost my kitchen last year. Oil fire. I wasn't even cooking. My ex decided to fry wings while watching a Raiders game."

"That's... ambitious."

"He threw water on an oil fire—as the flames were already licking the ceiling. Real problem solver."

Frank winced. "That's not just a fire, that's Darwinism."

Her laughter was short but real. It echoed off the laminated evacuation posters behind her.

After the class, while the usual trickle of attendees filed out, Nancy lingered. She wasn't awkward. She didn't overshare. She just folded her notebook, tucked it under her arm, and said:

"Thanks. Most people talk like they're reading a warning label. You didn't."

Frank nodded, suddenly unsure of himself in a room he'd stood in numerous times.

"Well… warning labels are in the advanced class. Just make sure your mattress still has one, or I'll have to call the Sealy police."

They both paused—caught in the strange silence of two people who didn't expect to notice each other.

She gestured toward the coffee urn in the corner.

"Any chance that sludge is still hot?"

"Hot, sure," Frank said. "Same way a dumpster fire is hot."

"Perfect," she said. "That's kind of my brand."

Nancy poured herself a cup of the suspiciously simmering

coffee and gave it a sniff like a mechanic evaluating motor oil.

"Well," she said, taking a small sip. "Not actively poisonous."

"That's the house blend," Frank said. "Hints of linoleum and unresolve."

She smiled over the rim of the paper cup. "I've had worse. My first job was at a pumpkin patch off 101, where they brewed coffee in a rusted percolator that probably hadn't been washed since Y2K. I'm basically immune."

"Let me guess—born and raised in NorCal?"

She nodded. "Petaluma. Cows, craft fairs, and too many second-hand bookstores. My mom still thinks tofu is witchcraft."

Frank leaned against the folding table, arms crossed. "And yet somehow, you survived."

"I learned to pack early," she said, tapping her neatly folded notebook. "I was the girl with extra granola bars and a printed map to the field trip."

He laughed. "You're a prepper."

"No," she said with a smirk, "I'm just allergic to chaos."

Frank raised an eyebrow. "Then what brought you to a fire safety class in a city built on chaos?"

"Divorce. New place. Fresh start." She shrugged. "And I light a lot of candles."

“Ah, pyromancy. The gateway to healing.”

She batted her eyes playfully and took another sip. “So, what’s your story, Fire Guy?”

Frank hesitated, his smile fading just slightly. “Ex-firefighter. Currently teaching and moonlighting as an Uber therapist. Recently replaced professionally—turns out even heroism has a shelf life.”

Nancy blinked. “Wow. Okay. Well… that beats my candle thing.”

He chuckled. “Sorry. That got darker than intended.”

“No,” she said, setting the cup down. “It got honest. I like that.”

There was a pause. Not awkward. Not unlike the moment before a curtain rises.

“Would you maybe want to grab something less flammable than coffee sometime?” Frank asked.

Nancy tilted her head. “You mean a date?”

“I mean… yeah. Unless that violates some sacred community center code of conduct.”

She smiled—dry, direct, but not unfriendly. “If I said no, you’d be the first fire safety instructor I’ve turned down this month.”

“Well then,” Frank said, surprised by the flicker in his chest, “I’ll take that as a yes.”

He handed her a temporary business card—creased, slightly smudged, but still legible.

Nancy shifted her notebook under her arm. "I'll text you. And Frank?"

"Yeah?"

"No instruction manuals."

She turned and walked out—calm, composed, and completely untouched by the spark she'd just set in motion. Frank stood there, blinking at the empty doorway, wondering what had just happened.

Then he smiled.

And for the first time in a long time, it wasn't bittersweet.

CHAPTER II

ONE STAR ENCOUNTERS

"People who smile while they are alone used to be called insane, until we invented smartphones and social media."

— MOKOKOMA MOKHONOANA

The kiss of the rising sun lit up the dashboard of the first-generation Prius, ushering to life the majestic Golden Gate Bridge. Below the iconic span, the wind whipped the bay waters into a white-capped fury.

For Frank Wright, a deep, cleansing breath was no longer about renewal—just a reset. Similar to turning the phone off and back on, hoping something changed. The night

before, he'd driven strangers across town, listened to their breakups, their rants, their silence.

Frank had just finished dropping off a couple who smelled like kombucha and weed when his app pinged again: **Pickup – The Mission District. 2 passengers.**

He rolled up slowly, half-listening to a podcast titled **Matched & Mismatched: Love in the Age of Algorithms,** when he saw her.

Stefania.

In the flesh—vintage band tee half-tucked into tattered blue jeans, high-top sneakers loose at the ankles. Her hair was pinned up with half a chopstick, and she was, undeniably, radiant.

She looked like she'd drifted straight out of his subconscious—half memory, half mirage.

Beside her stood a man in a neatly pressed white Oxford and tailored navy slacks, the sleeves pushed up just enough to look effortless. He had a clean-cut look, a quiet confidence, and a hint of cedar cologne that lingered without trying too hard. "Frank?" she said, leaning into the passenger window. "Is that you?"

An emotional sinkhole opened beneath him, but he managed a weak smile and muttered, "Yep. It's really me."

She climbed into the back with her companion.

"This is so random," Stefania said, as if randomness could erase the quiet, digital cold war that had developed. It had been a month since the viral axe throw—four weeks of ghosting. And now, somehow, the universe had arranged a rematch through a rideshare app.

The man leaned forward and offered a hand through the crack between the seats. "Namaste, man. I'm Tim Banks, but my friends call me River. Big fan of ride-share workers. You guys are like the arteries of the city."

Frank shook his hand—more out of reflex than warmth. "Glad to keep things circulating," he muttered.

River chuckled, then refocused on his phone, eyes skimming over jagged market graphs.

In the rearview mirror, Frank caught Stefania's eyes. She looked away, then looked back. There was something in her gaze—not flirtation, not guilt exactly—just a silent nudge. As if she were signaling the axe throw hadn't been a fluke, that maybe she'd screwed up. But was it just wishful thinking, or could he really read her unspoken language? She tried to smile. Frank didn't return it, but he didn't look away either.

The car rolled through the city's soft-lit streets, silhouettes of homelessness punctuating the canvas like forgotten brushstrokes. River never looked up, lost in his market app, oblivious to anything not glowing.

Stefania glanced at Frank again, her expression softer this time—half apology, half hope, or maybe nothing at all.

The moment bent with his perception, shifting as he tried to pin it down. And there it was: the familiar ache in his gut, the sense of something just out of reach. Almost.

When they pulled up to the curb, River hopped out first, still scrolling.

Stefania hesitated.

"Hey," she said quietly, leaning forward just a little. "It was... really good to see you again."

Frank nodded. "You too."

She lingered, as if on the edge of a sentence, then gently closed the door.

He watched her fade into the night through the rearview mirror, the ache still lodged in his stomach like a question mark he couldn't answer.

He didn't mark her as gone. Not yet.

Frank sat idle for a moment, the engine ticking softly in the quiet. Then his phone buzzed.

☆☆☆☆☆ – You were great.

From Stefania.

He stared at the screen longer than necessary, thumb hovering like the message might suddenly update itself.

Five stars.

Was it politeness? Nostalgia? Regret? Hope?

He didn't know.

Maybe it was just a rating. Maybe it was the last good thing she'd ever give him.

Or maybe—just maybe—it meant she hadn't closed the door either.

He set the phone down gently, shifted the car into drive, and pulled back into the stream of lights.

Traffic was light. The night hung loose and half-asleep. A warm breeze pressed against the windows like a sigh. He took the long way home without meaning to—winding through Dolores, down past the silent carousel at Golden Gate Park. Just movement. Just motion.

Another buzz.

He glanced down.

> Stefania: Hey… I wanted to explain. I know I disappeared, and I'm sorry. I went to Yellowstone right after our park greet. I needed space to recharge, to listen—to nature, mostly. To myself. I know that's not a great excuse. I just wasn't in a place to… connect. But I'm trying to be now. If you're open to talking, I'd like that.

Frank read it three times.

Yellowstone.

Of course, she went to Yellowstone.

He pictured her standing in some geothermal field, arms stretched toward a pastel sky, waiting for the earth to whisper something back. Maybe it had. Maybe she'd come back with enlightenment. Or maybe just better cell service.

He wanted to be angry. Wanted to type something about timing and ghosting and how human connection wasn't an app you could toggle on and off like Do Not Disturb mode.

But he didn't.

Instead, he set the phone face down on the passenger seat and gripped the wheel with both hands.

He was tired of being left.

Gail.

The firehouse.

Stefania.

One by one, they had all found exits. He was still circling the roundabout, hunting for a turnoff that wouldn't vanish the second he took it.

And yet… he wanted to believe her. Needed to believe something still tethered him to meaning. To someone. He didn't want to float anymore.

He wanted an anchor—anything to stop the slow, silent drift.

After a few blocks, he reached for the phone again. His thumb hovered for a long time.

Frank: I'm still here.

He stared at the message. It felt small, but honest. And that would have to be enough.

He hit send.

Then drove on, chasing the taillights in front of him as if they knew where to go.

CHAPTER 12
BOWLING FOR LAUGHS

"The illiterate of the 21st century will not be those who cannot read and write, but those who cannot learn, unlearn, and relearn."

— **ALVIN TOFFLER**, FUTURE SHOCK

The kiss of the rising sun lit up the dashboard of the first-generation Prius, ushering to life the majestic Golden Gate Bridge. Below the iconic span, the wind whipped the bay waters into a white-capped fury.

For Frank Wright, a deep, cleansing breath had become a daily ritual—similar to checking for cracks in a dam. But Ron? Ron was the crack. He knew chaos, had bathed in its

warm waters, and somehow emerged squeaky clean. His familiarity with turbulence afforded him a strange confidence, the kind possessed by someone who lived outside the rules. Armed with cologne, half-baked podcast theories, and dating profiles polished like résumés, he didn't just survive the shifting game—he thrived by winging it.

"Amigo. You're not gonna believe it—I crushed last night. Standing ovation. At a bowling alley."

Ron stood in his kitchen, shirtless and barefoot, holding a protein shake like it was a mic. Frank sat at the kitchen counter, still processing Stefania's five-star message, trying to decide whether it was a lifeline or a landmine.

"You're doing stand-up now?" Frank asked.

"Technically, yes. Spiritually, it's more like spoken-word truth bombs for people waiting on mozzarella sticks. The place is called *Split Happens*. It's a lounge attached to a bowling alley in San Mateo. Half the audience was drunk, and one guy heckled me in sign language. But I owned it."

Frank blinked. "This is a Tuesday night gig?"

"Tuesday is the new Saturday, amigo. The weekend crowds are a totally different demographic. They can't hear my voice. Tuesday people can hear me—they're just deaf. Plus, the manager comps me an hour of bowling."

Ron took a swig of his shake and flexed, unprovoked.

"Something strange happened last night when I went to pick up some people in the Mission District," Frank said cautiously.

Ron spilled his shake on his chest. "Please don't say it was Stefania."

Frank hesitated.

Ron dropped his arm. "No. No, no, no. Tell me you didn't pick up the ghost."

Frank shrugged. "She got in the car with some guy. Hedge fund type. Smelled like cedar and tax loopholes."

Ron groaned. "And you didn't pull over and fake an engine fire?"

"She was... different. Kept catching my eye in the mirror. Said it was good to see me."

"She also said nothing for weeks," Ron snapped. "Dude, this is textbook emotional re-targeting. You're a nostalgia ad in her head. Don't fall for it."

Frank looked down at his phone, Stefania's rating still glowing.

Five stars.

"Yeah," he said. "Maybe."

Ron grabbed his keys and pointed them like a weapon. "Don't *maybe* this. You need closure. Or garlic fries. Possibly both. You're going with me to *Split Happens* tonight. It's open mic night and I plan on doing a bit about your love life —working title: *Swiped and Ghosted: A Frank Tragedy.*"

Frank didn't argue. He'd learned long ago that when Ron had momentum, resistance was just part of the warm-up.

His mind drifted—back to junior high, back when his family moved upstate from a town so conservative even the dogs wore flag pins on the Fourth of July.

Frank had been the new kid with the tucked-in shirts and side-part haircut, dropped into a school where the social currency was sarcasm and skateboard brands. He barely lasted a week before the local pack of preteen jackals decided he looked like the inside of a church bulletin.

Ron saved him.

Literally stepped in between Frank and a kid nicknamed "Cinderblock" during lunch. Frank still remembered the exact words:

"He's with me. Back off, or I'll tell everyone your mom sells Amway!"

It worked.

The next day, Ron showed up with a beat-up windboard littered with surf decals and said, "You ever windsurf?"

Frank had no idea what it was.

Ron grinned. "Good. You'll learn faster."

That summer, Frank nearly drowned twice and caught a total of one wave while dodging seals. But it stuck.

Ron, a product of a single-dad household with a fridge full of condiments and zero vegetables, had been pulling Frank out of wrecks for years—bullies, bad outfits, bar romances, and now, emotional U-turns in the back seat of a hybrid.

"Tonight's gonna be magic. Or a total disaster. Either way, we'll get mozzarella sticks."

Frank shook his head and smiled. Stefania might be a question mark, but Ron was punctuation—the loud, ridiculous kind that never let the sentence end quietly.

As Ron began workshopping a new bowling lounge bit—something about emotional manipulation, the gamification of ghosting, and the rewards system for fractured dating—Frank only half listened.

His eyes drifted to the cluttered bookshelf across the room.

Wedged between a dog-eared copy of *The Game* and a spiral-bound stand-up notebook was Alvin Toffler's *Future Shock*—the only book from his two-year college experience that scared him.

He stared at the spine of *Future Shock*, the same way you might stare at a warning label after the damage is already done. Toffler's thesis was unnervingly simple: too much change, too fast, and the human psyche starts to bend in on itself. Not shatter—just quietly fold under the pressure of constant acceleration. Progress without pause.

Back then, it sounded theoretical. Now, Frank was living it. Love, once a slow bloom, had been replaced by instant compatibility scores and disappearing messages. Intimacy arrived via pop-up, expired like produce. Who needed commitment when you could engineer connection? Artificial wombs, designer embryos—it all sounded like science fiction until he found himself dog-paddling through the deep end of modern courtship, gasping for something real. Maybe he wasn't heartbroken. Maybe he was just outdated.

Ron was still rambling nearby—something about Stefania's star rating being a trap.

"Five stars, Frank? That's not closure, it's bait!"

But Frank kept his eyes on *Future Shock*, feeling a quiet hum of recognition. It wasn't just Stefania. It was everything: his job, his identity, his instincts—caught in the spin cycle of modern life. He wanted to hit pause. Or eject. Or at least skip ahead to the part where he knew what the hell he was doing.

Instead, he asked, "You think I'm still in it with her?"

Ron didn't hesitate. "You're not just in it. You're drowning in shallow water."

Frank exhaled through his nose. Maybe. Or maybe he was just a man trying to make sense of a future that no longer asked permission.

And then, predictably, Ron kicked open the moment like a drunken rodeo clown.

"Amigo! I forgot to tell you," he shouted, slapping a bowling score sheet on the counter. "Tammy Lynn came with me. And she was pure smoke—rhinestone jeans, rodeo hair, and a wicked bowling game that makes the balls scream for mercy."

Frank blinked. "What?"

"She bowls league—F'in certified. She even has a bowling pin tattoo on the small of her back that glimmers when she follows through!"

"Shocking."

Ron powered through. "She heckled me during my set last night, right after I made a joke about emotional support seals. Said I reminded her of her second ex-husband, but funnier and with fewer restraining orders. Then she challenged me to a bowl-off and promised line dancing if I broke a hundred."

Frank smirked. "Did you?"

"Eighty-six. But I talked fast, and she was two margaritas in. We ended up reenacting *9½ Weeks* at her place—only with jalapeños instead of ice."

Frank opened his mouth, ready to mention Stefania—the mirror glances, the questions that hadn't quite left.

But Ron steamrolled ahead.

"Oh! And she even taught me how to say 'no strings attached' in a Texas accent—like I was born in a honky-tonk and raised on brisket. Frank, I'm telling you—she's the swipe of my life. I thought love was a mirage. Turns out it just moved from Ft. Worth and changed its name to Tammy Lynn."

Frank sighed. "She gave me five stars...."

Ron waved him off. "Nope. Not today, Satan. Don't throw that mojo at me. This is a Stefania-free zone. "I've got a potential love triangle brewing between a woman with Dairy Queen and bowling pin tattoos and a person who stayed after my set to ask for merch. You and your haunted match can wait their turn."

Frank leaned back in the chair, nursing a warm hard seltzer.

Maybe Toffler was right. The future wasn't just arriving fast —it was barreling down the lane, picking off pins, one heart at a time.

Ron began to pace.

"Bro," Ron said, snapping his fingers, "you've been looking at this all wrong. You can't keep trying to appeal to women like they're reading résumés. That's not attraction—that's HR. You need a system. A framework. I call mine the Pyramid of Attraction."

Frank squinted. "Didn't you already pitch that once? I thought it was called the Pyramid of Swipes."

Ron grinned, unbothered. "Different levels, same science. The Pyramid of Swipes is about volume—how many profiles you churn through before you hit gold. The

Pyramid of Attraction is about *quality control.* It's the next evolution."

Frank leaned back, unimpressed. "So, what—you went from counting bodies to building one?"

Ron ignored the jab, sketching a triangle in the air with his fingers. "Top tier—bikinis beat cross-eyes every time. Mid-tier—women with no kids beat women with ugly kids. Women with ugly kids beat women with no sense of humor. Survival of the hottest, the youngest, the least complicated."

Frank snorted. "Sounds more like the survival of your delusions."

Ron smirked. "Hey, nature doesn't swipe left—it just selects."

"Alright, listen," Ron began, holding up one finger like he was about to unveil a trade secret. "It's a pyramid. Top tier? Best-looking guy. Always gets the first look. No mystery there."

"Go on," Frank said dryly.

Ron smirked. "If Pretty Boy's broke, the floor drops out. That's when personality has a shot—the funny guy, the poet, the dad-bod philosopher who makes her laugh. But you?" He jabbed a finger. "You're still top tier—good-looking guy. Problem is, you're driving Uber now. That drops you halfway down the pyramid."

Frank took a drink. "So basically, I'm a handsome downgrade with car air fresheners."

Ron grabbed a fistful of Taco Bell napkins and started scribbling like he was mapping treasure. "See, amigo, you used to be on the north side of the pyramid—handsome guy with a steady job. Solid tier. But now? Still good looks, sure, but unemployed? You've slid down a notch."

He held up the napkin, a crooked triangle with messy arrows. "Top of the heap? Handsome ***and*** rich. Or famous. Celebrity, cult leader, whatever—status wins. Next tier down: steady work guy with muscles. Firefighter, contractor, cop—any dude who looks like he can lift a couch without throwing out his back. Then below that? Home Depot guy with a peg leg. Not handsome, not rich, but dependable. Won't cheat—he's too busy buying wood screws and limping to the truck."

Ron jabbed the napkin with his pen. "That's the pyramid. And the rest? Poets, funny guys, Uber drivers with five stars —they live in the margins. Women aren't picking jokes, my dude. They're picking the guy they want in the Instagram photo."

Frank frowned. "That's bleak. What about bad boys? Motorcycle guys, wrestler villains, the tattooed man-bun crowd?"

Ron drew another crooked tier across the napkin. "Ah, the chaos bracket. They don't even fit in the pyramid—they orbit it. Short-term gravitational pull. Motorcycle guy, ex-con with abs, amateur wrestler who drinks tequila for breakfast. They're the human fireworks show. Loud, explosive, burns out quick—but they get their window."

He leaned back, satisfied. "Women dabble in bad boys the way people dabble in extreme sports. Thrilling for a weekend, but nobody wants season tickets."

"Go back to the celebrity tier..." Frank said, eyeing the mess of napkins with a mix of skepticism and curiosity. "You're telling me some county-fair Elton John impersonator outranks a six-figure union guy with benefits?"

Ron lit up, scribbling harder. "Every day of the week. Doesn't even have to be a ***real*** celebrity. Cover band frontman, local weatherman, the dude who almost won ***Worst Cooks in America.*** Boom—he leapfrogs the handsome plumber with a pension plan."

Frank shook his head, half amused. "So Rocket Man in rhinestones gets the date, while the guy who can actually pay the mortgage gets friend-zoned."

Ron jabbed the napkin. "Exactly. Why? Perceived access. Status. Clout. He's not just a guy—he's a symbol. Women chase symbols."

Frank exhaled. "That's not a pyramid—it seems more like a house of mirrors, with every angle a distortion."

Ron leaned in, voice low. "Yeah—and in your mirror, the distortion had darker skin and your job in his pocket."

Frank leaned back, eyes on the ceiling. "I used to run into burning buildings."

Ron clapped him on the shoulder. "Exactly. You *did*. Now

you drive Uber and sleep in my vape cloud. We gotta repackage you."

Frank groaned. "Ughh, someone please help me."

Ron grinned. "Don't worry. I've got a plan. You're gonna be a myth by the end of this. A legend. A dating app Loch Ness Monster."

Frank closed his eyes. "Just promise me I don't have to sing 'Rocket Man' in a sequin blazer."

"No promises, my dude."

CHAPTER 13

STAR-CROSSED LOVERS

"Fate leads the willing and drags the unwilling."

— **SENECA,** *LETTERS TO LUCILIUS*

The kiss of the rising sun lit up the dashboard of the first-generation Prius, ushering to life the majestic Golden Gate Bridge. Below the iconic span, the wind whipped the bay waters into a white-capped fury.

For Frank Wright, a deep, cleansing breath had once signaled a clean slate. Now it felt the way holding his breath did before the next twist.

Frank adjusted his faded department-issued polo and tugged at the collar like it might hide the fact that he hadn't slept. He stood at the front of the rec center classroom, watching the handful of participants trickle in. Retirees, a young mom with a stroller, a guy in cargo shorts who kept calling it "fight club for fire."

Then, right on time—Nancy.

She entered with her usual unhurried grace, wearing a burnt-orange San Francisco Giants windbreaker and holding a stainless-steel coffee tumbler like it was a sacrament to the morning. Her eyes found Frank, and the corners of her mouth lifted. Not a grin, but something more than surface.

"Back again?" he asked, leaning casually against the folding table piled with outdated CPR dummies.

"Someone has to keep you honest," she replied. "Besides, last week's lesson on grease fires? Life-changing. I haven't used my air fryer since."

Frank chuckled. It was the first laugh he'd had in days—maybe because he was still emotionally hungover from Ron's standup set, a twenty-minute descent into dating app purgatory that felt similar to watching a man confess to a murder he hadn't committed.

Behind him, the fight club guy was windmilling punches at a CPR dummy, shouting, "Make me come to this crap on my day off now, Mr. Powell!" No one stopped him. Honestly, it all made sense to Frank.

"By the way," Nancy said, sipping from her tumbler, "sorry I bailed on that drink earlier this week. Minor girlfriend-group crisis—Greece trip planning. Three meltdowns in one night: Airbnb drama, luggage limits, and whether goat yogurt qualifies as cultural immersion."

Frank smiled. "Sounds intense."

"Oh, it was. One of them threatened to cancel unless we all agreed to wear matching linen. I had to mediate like it was the United Nations of divorcees."

Frank smiled and then glanced at the clock as the session began. He moved through his usual rhythm—the anatomy of a fire extinguisher, why you don't throw water on a pan fire unless you want to star in your own viral kitchen disaster. But as he spoke, his eyes kept drifting to Nancy.

When he asked for a volunteer for a two-person fire escape drill, she stood without hesitation.

They moved through the scenario—Frank narrating, Nancy improvising. The space between them shrank with every step. At one point, she reached instinctively for his wrist to guide him toward the imaginary exit.

It was a small thing.

But to Frank, it felt like a defibrillator to the chest.

After class, while the others clustered near the vending machines, arguing over Funyuns versus granola bars, Nancy lingered. She didn't fidget or pretend to check her phone—

she simply waited, eyes fixed on him with a kind of quiet intent.

When he finally looked up, she tilted her head, a playful smile tugging at her lips. "You know…they say touch is the strongest love language. When you grabbed my hand during that fire drill—" she let the thought dangle, her gaze holding his a beat longer than expected, "—I almost forgot we were supposed to be escaping."

Frank felt his throat catch. He coughed, stalling for time, then decided to quit hedging. "You doing anything Thursday night?"

She raised an eyebrow. "Depends. Will there be fire extinguishers involved?"

"Only if things go really well," he said with a straight face.

She laughed—really laughed—and gave him a nod.

"Alright, Fireman Frank. You've got yourself a maybe."

Frank watched her walk off, that same easy, confident stride like she'd never once tripped over her own uncertainty. The classroom emptied slowly, except for the fight club guy, who was now on the floor nursing a black eye after somehow managing to catch a full rebound from the CPR dummy. He limped out muttering something about his boss winning again.

As Frank walked to his car, a half-smile tugged at him. For once, in a long while, he wasn't scrounging for Cupid's leftovers. It felt like hope—real, unfiltered, maybe even a sign.

Then a voice—soft, familiar, laced with uncertainty—cut through the late morning.

"Frank."

He turned. Stefania stood by the passenger side of his Prius, arms open, her face unreadable.

"She's nice," she said, as an observation—logging it away. "And pretty, too."

Frank blinked. "Stefania... what are you doing here? Where did you come from?"

"I remembered you mentioned your class last week during the Uber ride," she said, stepping closer. "And then I saw Orion's Belt the night of the ride, and it felt like a sign."

He blinked again, slower this time.

"Now, you believe in fate?" Frank asked, half-skeptical.

"I believe in the stars," she said calmly. "Signs. Energy. Timing. And I believe not everything ends because it's supposed to. Sometimes it's just… a hiccup."

Frank looked down. "You ghosted me. That's more than a hiccup."

"I know," she said without flinching. "And I own that. But maybe it was needed—a reset of sorts. A cosmic cleansing breath."

She glanced toward the rec center, then back at him with a half-smile that hid her real thoughts.

"Is she what you're interested in?" she asked, tilting her head slightly. "Someone steady? Simple?" She paused, her voice softening. "She seems nice. The kind of person who has a plan for everything. Probably meal preps with Pinterest and has *Hallmark* movies memorized."

She stepped closer, her voice dipping into something softer —intimate, maybe even sincere.

"But you and I both know... pleasant doesn't keep you up at night. Pleasant doesn't make you question the world, or make you scream when throwing axes."

Frank felt something shift in his chest—something between a warning, a want, or a beginning coronary.

Stefania smiled, slow and sly, like a tarot card turned over at just the right moment.

She looked away for a moment, then back at him.

"She's... pleasant. Easy to be around. And maybe that's exactly what you need right now."

There was no bitterness in her tone—just a hint of something quieter. Maybe longing. Maybe loss.

Frank exhaled slowly. Stefania's words always hovered between insight and enigma. She followed signs; he followed streetlights. Yet something about her tugged at him—quiet, persistent. She looked at him not with pressure, but with pull.

"I'm not here to complicate anything," she said gently. "Just… maybe a conversation. Or at least trying to figure out our stars."

Frank looked at her for a long moment. He wasn't sure what he believed anymore—about people, about timing, about what any of it meant. Most days, he felt like he was still sorting through pieces with no clear picture.

"I don't know," he said honestly. "I've been on a roller coaster for a while."

She gave a small nod, as if she'd expected as much. "That's fair."

No pressure. No insistence.

Stefania stepped back, giving him space. "If the timing's right, you'll know. If not... that's okay too."

She offered a quiet smile—just enough to register—and turned to go, her steps unhurried, her presence lingering in the space she left behind.

Frank stayed there, rooted in place, watching her fade into the soft blur of the street. He didn't know if he'd just side-stepped something that might've undone him, or brushed past something that still had weight. Maybe it was both. Maybe that was okay.

A breeze swept in, carrying the scent of city dust and salt water. He looked up. The sun was steady overhead, clear and indifferent. Whatever the stars might've thought, they stayed hidden—silent for now.

CHAPTER 14

HOLLYWOOD SWINGING

"Politics is the art of looking for trouble, finding it everywhere, diagnosing it incorrectly, and applying the wrong remedies."

— GROUCHO MARX

The kiss of the rising sun lit up the dashboard of the first-generation Prius, ushering to life the majestic Golden Gate Bridge. Below the iconic span, the wind whipped the bay waters into a white-capped fury.

For Frank Wright, a deep, cleansing breath used to mean readiness. Now it was just reflex. Somewhere down south, his wife was smiling for cameras next to a man who had taken his job, his cat's loyalty, and now his place

in the narrative. Frank was no longer part of the story. He was the cut line, the scene left on the floor.

Gail sat frozen on the edge of her queen bed—the one she used to share with Frank. The pale blue glow of her phone lit the darkened room, making her loneliness undeniable. Mayor Apple's latest campaign post was still on the screen: a photo of her and Javier laughing beneath a banner that read Tomorrow's California—Rooted in Change.

The caption below it was worse than the image itself: FAMILY IS EVOLVING. SO IS CALIFORNIA.

Her stomach turned.

It wasn't just the photo—it was the memory snapping into place, similar to a wine-soaked puzzle piece. The barbecue. Jax's birthday. The mayor's assistants, too friendly by design, circling with curated enthusiasm and rehearsed warmth. Their smiles never slipped, their hands always carrying another glass of chilled chardonnay. The third had felt celebratory at the time. Liberating, even.

And then there was Javier—tall, easy-smiling, wearing a faded Station 11 shirt and the scent of sandalwood and summer. He looked enough like Frank to disarm her, but with that added Latin allure, as if someone had edited her ex-husband through a romance filter. One moment, she was laughing at some harmless comment about firehouse food, the next, she was swaying in his arms to a Bluetooth speaker playing Marvin Gaye.

She exhaled slowly.

Later, one of her neighbors suggested that Apple's assistants hadn't just happened to be there—they were sent. Told to open the door to the possible. Told to "let things unfold organically," which, in campaign-speak, meant gently manipulating the optics until Gail was wrapped around a man the mayor could package as progressive proof-of-concept.

She stared at the screen. There was Apple again, mid-laugh, clinking glasses with a carefully diverse circle of supporters. *California's future,* engineered as a PR stunt—and she'd played her part perfectly.

Gail thought out loud, "How did I get here?"

Her life had been a freefall—Frank gone, the bills multiplying, and prior to Javier, the silence in the house thick enough to chew. Then Mayor Apple began dropping by with her latte in hand and those perfectly timed words of encouragement, it had felt… nice. As if someone was finally paying attention.

"You're part of something bigger now," Apple had said once, her tone equal parts warmth and polished ambition. "The world is watching, Gail. Women like us—we shape what they see."

It was flattering. It was terrifying. And for someone whose life had just imploded, it was an intoxicating kind of purpose.

It was all too much to digest. The room was haunting. She started to cry, then stopped herself.

She sank back onto the bed, unsure whether she was resting or surrendering.

Maybe both.

Gail let the phone fall to the carpet. She wasn't sure what hurt more—betraying the bond, or how easily she'd slipped under suggestion.

She wasn't one to linger in self-pity. At the next round of dings, she picked up the phone. Three unread texts from Frank—the first in a long time. Each, some version of *Can we talk?* Before Jax's barbecue, he'd tried relentlessly—calls, emails, texts—all ignored.

Gail told herself she needed space. That silence was clarity. But the truth sat heavier now. She hadn't answered because she didn't know how. The break was supposed to be temporary, a moment to breathe, recalibrate. But it had steamrolled into something unrecognizable the moment Javier brought his duffel bag inside and started cooking with hot sauce.

Now there were campaign photographers scheduled. A stylist texting about earth-tone wardrobe options. And Gail—somehow—had been recast as the symbol of modern reinvention in a state that prided itself on progressive optics.

Her silence wasn't strength. It was avoidance.

Outside, the fog curled in like a soft gray carpet, blanketing the area in its usual coastal hush. At the end of the cul-de-sac, Mayor Apple's electric SUV glided silently into the driveway of the Wright home.

Technically, it was still *their* address. But only half of them lived there now. And the other half kept asking if they could talk.

As the fog began to lift, the house stood quiet, almost serene. A glass-fronted jewel overlooking the bay, framed by coastal rosemary and the faint sight of sailboats drifting out with the tide.

It wasn't supposed to be in reach for a firefighter and a homemaker's wife. But then again, most people hadn't pulled a tech billionaire out of a burning lithium-ion yacht.

Frank had.

The story never made the news—at the billionaire's request—but the gratitude had been real. A quiet thank-you. A firm handshake. And a connection to a boutique lending group that specialized in "heroic optics." The kind of mortgage reserved for founders, disruptors, and the rare public servant with a near-death rescue on his résumé.

The deal had been absurdly favorable. Frank had hesitated. Gail hadn't.

Now Frank was gone, and the house remained—echoing with the soft click of her phone and the question that still hung in the air.

Can we talk?

In the backyard, Javier ran in chaotic circles with a garden hose slung over his shoulder, barking commands in Spanish and making siren noises between gulps of air. The hose flopped behind him like a reluctant tail. On the pergola above, TC—the aging Maine Coon Frank once called his "spiritual advisor"—watched with the disinterest of a Zen monk, tail flicking, expression unreadable.

The backyard gate groaned open. Mayor Apple stepped into the scene like a choreographed entrance on a political talk show. Designer pumps. Shimmer-blazer. Hair and makeup that somehow thrived in the coastal gloom. Pixel, her data whisperer in oversized glasses and neutral tones, followed at a respectful distance.

She breezed past the rosemary planter, strutting as if paparazzi were hidden in the shrubbery, and let herself into the yard without knocking—because people like her hadn't knocked in years.

"Gail!" she called out, "I have *such* good news."

Gail had emerged from the bedroom, wiping away lingering tears with a tissue, brows already suspiciously arched.

Apple pointed toward the lawn, where Javier was now crawling on one knee, spraying mist into the air like a fire safety demo for imaginary children. "He's adorable. A little public servant in training. Firefighter cosplay is *so* in right now."

Javier spun and accidentally sprayed a jet of water near Apple's shoes. She sidestepped like a Broadway dancer and laughed. "Spirited. I like it."

"What's going on?" Gail asked, already bracing for the inevitable pitch.

"I want you and Javier to come with me. Southern California tour. A few campaign stops, some visibility with our diversity-forward family unit. We'll hit Los Angeles, San Diego, maybe Palm Springs... something breezy but strategic."

Gail blinked. "A political tour?"

"Yes, think policy meets influencer culture." Apple's thumbs danced across her phone. "We'll swing by the set of *Malibu Undercover*—you know, that sun-soaked crime drama where lifeguards moonlight as detectives. You and Javier could cameo as climate refugees. Very topical. Very... us."

TC yawned from his perch.

"There's also a Hollywood party next week," Apple continued. "The 21st Century Wives of Rodeo Drive are launching their reboot. Think Botox, borrowed jewelry, and empowerment."

Gail folded her arms. "Seriously?"

"Of course," Apple said. "The optics are perfect. You're a brave, intelligent woman navigating life after a traditional marriage collapse. He's... well, he's photogenic, semi-bilingual, and simple. That's everything we want in a redemption narrative." Gail's voice dropped. "And Frank?"

Apple waved a hand like swatting away a fruit fly. "What about Frank? He's stuck in a rec center from what I'm told —still trying to learn, unlearn, and relearn the 21st century."

She stepped forward, lowering her voice like it was supposed to sound intimate and not transactional. "You? You're forward-facing. You're the now."

Out in the yard, Javier gave a proud salute with the garden hose and slipped on a wet patch of grass, landing squarely on his backside with a squeal.

Apple clapped once. "See? Authentic."

Suddenly, Javier gave a proud salute with the garden hose. The nozzle slipped, and a sharp burst of water shot directly at Mayor Apple's sunglasses.

She yelped, then laughed, dabbing her face with the sleeve of her shimmer-blazer. "See? Moments like this—that's the story. A new kind of California."

Gail managed a tight smile, but her thoughts were elsewhere. Frank wasn't some relic of a fading world. He was still calling. Still trying. And she had let the silence do the work of separation.

Pixel, standing just behind the conversation with tablet in hand, leaned in discreetly.

"Mayor," she murmured, "we're running twelve minutes behind."

Apple exhaled, dabbing her glasses one last time, then squared her shoulders. "Right. Let's make some democracy."

Javier resumed his heroic routine, spraying invisible flames with theatrical urgency. TC, meanwhile, had zero interest in the show. His eyes locked on a lizard sunning itself beneath Frank's old grill.

With the precision of a furry assassin, the Maine Coon leapt from the pergola and landed with a thud. The lizard vanished. A rusty spatula clattered to the patio as TC dove after it, wedging himself halfway under the grill, his tail twitching like a pinball machine in tilt.

Mayor Apple jumped. "What was that?"

"Just the cat chasing small reptiles," Gail said, her eyes still on the yard, her tone flat.

Pixel glanced at their screen. "We're now thirteen minutes behind."

Apple turned back to Gail, her sunglasses still dripping. She smiled that perfectly rehearsed campaign smile.

"So? Are you in? California's waiting."

That night, the house was quiet in a way that made Gail feel as if she were a guest in her own life.

Gail sat curled on the edge of the couch, a worn shoebox open on the coffee table in front of her. Inside—faded photographs, old postcards, a napkin from their first real date in North Beach with a doodle Frank had drawn of her as a stick figure and huge smile. Her thumb traced the edges of one photo: Frank, younger and leaner, arms slung around her shoulders in front of a rust-colored barn in Manhattan, Kansas. Her childhood home. She was nineteen, barefoot in the grass, laughing at something he'd just whispered in her ear just before proposing. She smiled, thinking about her family's response to the news after meeting Frank for the first time.

Back then, she was still Gail Williams. A Midwest girl with straight A's and a full ride to Stanford. And then came Frank Wright—Northern California strong, silly with charm, stubborn integrity. He had that old-school steadiness that reminded her of home, of wheat fields and porch swings and the kind of love that didn't need disclaimers.

She gave up everything for him. Not in bitterness. In belief.

In the next room, Javier yelled something in Spanish at the TV. The sound of foot meeting ball blasted through the surround sound, then a whistle. He was in Frank's man cave, legs kicked up on the same ottoman where Frank used to drink beer and scream at the Giants bullpen. Now Javier was screaming at Real Madrid and texting a cousin during commercial breaks. He hadn't even asked about the framed medals on the wall.

Gail sighed and leaned back, the photo still in her lap.

Had she crossed the line? Was there a point where silence stopped being a boundary and started becoming betrayal?

Her phone buzzed beside her.

> Pixel: Los Angeles itinerary locked. You + Javier needed for San Diego brunch, Malibu Undercover walk-thru, and the evening gala at the Beverly Hills Hotel. Wardrobe theme: 'Soft Power.' Car picks up at 5:40 a.m.

She stared at the text.

Soft power.

She turned back to the box of photos, as if one might answer her.

Or remind her what she used to believe in.

CHAPTER 15
BAR TAPS AND TABS

"Sex relieves tension—love causes it."

— WOODY ALLEN

The kiss of the rising sun lit up the dashboard of the first-generation Prius, ushering to life the majestic Golden Gate Bridge. Below the iconic span, the wind whipped the bay waters into a white-capped fury.

For Frank Wright, a deep, cleansing breath wasn't working today. His shirt smelled of fabric softener and someone else's choices. He'd been searching for warmth and found friction. It was connection, sure. But like all things lately, it came with a question mark.

Now, that same man stood in front of an open fridge in Oakland, squinting at a single yogurt cup and half a lime like they were the jury in a trial about his poor life choices. He closed the fridge with the gentle resignation of a man who already knew the verdict.

His bank app had confirmed what he'd been avoiding all week: two digits in the checking account. Three, if you included the decimal.

In the living room, Ron sat cross-legged on his beige beanbag chair, eating cereal out of a Tupperware bowl. A sliced jalapeño floated ominously near the edge. His eyes were fixed on a video titled *How to Market Yourself as a High-Value Man in the Age of Low Value.*

Frank plopped onto the couch, exhaling like a deflated air mattress.

"How much money do I need to stop pretending I'm not broke?" he asked, eyes on the ceiling.

Ron didn't look up. "Enough to buy a second yogurt, probably."

Frank rubbed his face. "Why do I keep swiping, man? I can't afford to date. I can barely afford to exist."

Ron set down his spoon as if he were about to give a TED Talk. "Because you're not swiping for women. You're swiping for proof."

Frank glanced over. "Proof?"

"Proof you're still wanted. Proof you're still alive. Proof you're still a man!"

Frank stared, hollow and half-impressed.

"And because running from despair is for cowards," Ron added. "You gotta run to it. That's where the power is."

Frank leaned back, absorbing that.

"You should put that on a T-shirt."

Ron smirked and resumed his breakfast, spoon clinking against the plastic like punctuation.

Later that day, Frank stood outside the rec center and texted Nancy. She replied almost instantly.

> Nancy: Let's do a little wine bar I love—super cute, kind of vibey.

Super cute. Kind of vibey. Also: probably expensive.

Frank stared at the message for a moment. His thumb hovered. His gut tensed.

But he wasn't about to bail.

Not after Ron's ridiculous gospel about swiping for proof and chasing despair like it owed you rent.

He would power through this date, a true man of purpose—and a man of hidden beverages.

Before leaving, Frank slid two wine coolers into the inside pockets of his well-worn field coat—the olive one with flannel lining and years of city fog baked into its seams. The bottles clinked softly, a glassy betrayal he tried to muffle with a strategic tug of the fabric. Zipping it felt too suspicious, too final, so he left it hanging just loose enough to suggest nonchalance.

He stepped back, studied himself in the mirror. Casual. Balanced. A man sneaking malt beverages into a boutique bar where cocktails answered to names like Moon Beam, and the garnish alone cost more than rent in Oakland.

Nancy had picked the place—one of those stylish spots with hanging Edison bulbs and reclaimed wood beams that gave off a curated rustic vibe. The wine list was printed on thick, textured paper that had been hand-pressed by monks with trust funds. She waved to Frank from a corner booth, already mid-sip of something chilled and faintly golden.

Frank slid into the booth across from her, adjusting his jacket as if it contained state secrets.

"This place is so intimate, right?" Nancy said, scanning the room. "Vintage smells and old San Francisco money."

Frank smirked. "Yeah. Like a therapy session built on a fault line—feels elegant, but one good tremor and the whole thing crumbles."

She laughed, settling in. When the server arrived, Frank ordered a sparkling water with the solemnity of someone who'd just read half an article on gut health.

"I'm cleansing," he said. "Or at least pretending to."

Nancy blinked, caught off guard. "Oh—I didn't realize. I was just about to order another sauvignon… I hope that's not a problem."

"No, it's fine," Frank said. "I'm just trying to avoid anything that tastes like it came out of a rec center vending machine."

She flashed an infectious smile, then let her right hand drift to the neckline of her blouse, smoothing the fabric with an almost absent elegance—subtle, but not accidental.

The drinks arrived—hers, chilled and light golden; his, politely fizzing as if it had good manners. Frank lifted his glass in mock ceremony. "Nothing says California romance like carbonated tap water," he quipped.

Conversation eased into a comfortable rhythm: updates on TC, complaints about eternal sidewalk repairs, and a neighbor who spent his retirement writing angry letters to the *Chronicle* about the slow death of San Francisco.

Nancy was engaged, relaxed—her eyes even lit up as she admitted a soft spot for Elvis and Hallmark movies.

Suddenly, Frank raised his glass again, this time with more conviction. "To no fires—except the kind started by love, cheap wine, or really good takeout."

Nancy clinked her glass against his with a grin. "Two out of three so far."

They clinked.

Frank took a sip, then tilted his head. "You said it was wings, right? The great kitchen inferno?"

Nancy groaned, smiling. "Wow, that story's never going away, is it?"

"You handed it to me," he said, grinning. "Ex-husband, Raiders game, hot oil, zero judgment."

"Fifteen years married," she said, shaking her head. "No kids —just a former cop with a deep fryer and a death wish for common sense."

Frank felt the line land harder than she knew. Eighteen years for him. No kids either. Different story, same math. For a flicker of a moment, their losses seemed to recognize each other.

After a small lull, Frank excused himself with a sheepish grin. "Quick pit stop."

In the restroom, he slipped a wine cooler from his jacket, as if it were a secret he wasn't proud of. He twisted the cap with quiet urgency and downed it in three gulps—the way a man swallows shame.

It tasted of necessity and blueberry, with a faint aftertaste of skid row. Pathetic, maybe—but free.

And in that moment—slightly buzzed, broke, and hiding contraband in a bar with a woman who collected Elvis coasters—Frank Wright felt oddly present. Or maybe just dizzy. Hard to tell.

Either way, he was still in the game.

He just had to survive the check.

As the night mellowed, their conversation drifted back toward legendary entertainers. Nancy lit up talking about Sinatra and Judy Garland, her hands animated, eyes shining as she recounted old performances like they were family memories. Frank played along, nodding in rhythm, offering the occasional well-timed Dean Martin reference.

"Any guy that can sing half asleep is aces in my book," he joked.

Nancy laughed, swirling the last of her wine, clearly charmed. She tilted her glass toward him. "Aces? Haven't heard that one in a while. You really are an old soul, Frank."

Later, Frank excused himself again—"Back in a flash"—and made his way to the restroom. There, under the hum of too-bright lights, he cracked open the second wine cooler with the stealth of a man who had nothing to lose and everything to hydrate. He downed it again in three gulps, his new ritual. Out of habit more than interest, he opened his dating app. A few empty swipes, nothing promising. Just noise.

He splashed water on his face, stared at his reflection in the mirror, and muttered, "You're doing great, I think," before heading back out like a half-sober gladiator re-entering the arena.

When he returned to the table, Nancy was waving off the server.

"Already took care of it," she said, sliding her card back into her purse with the ease of someone who didn't need a financial cleanse.

Frank blinked. "You sure?"

"Next time, it's yours," she said with a playful smile.

Riding the quiet rush of two covert wine coolers and a flicker of optimism, Frank leaned in just slightly.

"So," he said, casual but brave enough, "you wanna keep this going? I mean... if you're up for it."

Nancy studied him for a beat, then smiled. "Sure. Why not? But I have to—"

He didn't let her finish.

Frank pulled out his phone and texted for a ride. Not through the app. He messaged Rick—his semi-employed buddy who drove part-time and still owed him a favor from a botched poker night that ended with someone crying and a broken coffee table.

Ten minutes later, they slid into the back of a Toyota Corolla that smelled of gym socks and cinnamon gum. Rick caught their eyes in the rearview and winked.

"Meter's off tonight, brother. Just leave me five stars and a clean backseat."

Frank gave a grateful nod, settling in with the quiet satisfaction of a man who'd just cleared an invisible hurdle.

Her place was a cozy two-bedroom tucked into an aging duplex just north of downtown—the kind of building with creaky stairs, thin walls, and stubborn charm. The moment they stepped inside, Frank was greeted by the unmistakable gaze of The King—Elvis in full velvet glory, mid-hip swivel, arms outstretched as if blessing the room.

"I wasn't kidding about being a fan," Nancy said, slipping off her shoes. "He's my security system."

Frank grinned, taking it all in. The apartment felt like a time capsule wrapped in perfume and nostalgia. And somehow, it worked—framed concert posters, record sleeves in gold trim, and throw pillows that read *Taking Care of Business* in cursive rhinestones. The whole place hummed with a kind of unapologetic personality.

They stood in the soft glow of lamplight spilling through the open shades in the living room, both suspended in a moment that felt too intentional to be accidental.

Then Frank leaned in.

The kiss was soft, hesitant—but real. The first in nearly twenty years that hadn't belonged to Gail. He didn't register that fact until halfway through, when Nancy's hand rose gently to his chest. Desire stirred, slow and unfamiliar. But so did guilt. He was caught—between the ghost of a barely breathing marriage and the very real, very present woman now pulling him closer.

His wedding ring was somewhere in a junk drawer back in Oakland, buried under spare keys, expired coupons, and a mini flashlight that didn't work. Still, he felt its phantom weight pressing into his skin.

Nancy leaned in again, breath warm with wine and possibility. Somewhere deep inside, Frank's conscience mumbled something about vows, history, sacred bonds. But it sounded far away, like it was coming from underwater—or worse, from one of Gail's new wellness podcasts.

And still, he didn't stop.

Because the truth was, the marriage had flatlined a long time ago. Gail just hadn't signed the death certificate.

And Frank—well, Frank had always been bad with paperwork.

Morning light slipped through the thin curtains in Nancy's bedroom, giving everything a soft, easy glow. From the kitchen, he could hear her humming—barefoot, moving without rush. She poured coffee from a French press as though it were a sacred ritual, calm and unbothered. Frank watched from the hallway, thinking she resembled someone who hadn't just woken up, but reset.

As Frank moved to the edge of the couch, he tugged on his socks as if they owed him an apology. His shirt reeked of guilt and wine cooler. He checked his phone—no texts. Still, he felt accused.

"Sleep okay?" Nancy asked, sliding him a mug like they were two people at the beginning of something.

"Yeah. Great," Frank croaked. "Like a teenager. With a mortgage. And back pain."

She laughed and turned to rinse a few already-clean dishes, staying busy as though she was trying not to disrupt the illusion.

Frank forced a smile, grateful Nancy hadn't asked him to stay longer—or worse, to talk.

Five minutes later, he stepped out the door, the sun far too bright for someone still digesting shame and bar pretzels. A jogger passed, nodded. Frank nodded back, hoping he didn't see anyone he knew.

This was the updated walk of shame: no smeared eyeliner, no stilettos in hand—just a middle-aged man in sneakers and last night's cologne, trudging toward the horizon like a divorced pilgrim, half-hoping modern intimacy came with a punch card.

Five dates, get your manhood back.

CHAPTER 16
DOUBLE TROUBLE

"Be yourself; everyone else is already taken."

— OSCAR WILDE

The kiss of the rising sun lit up the dashboard of the first-generation Prius, ushering to life the majestic Golden Gate Bridge. Below the iconic span, the wind whipped the bay waters into a white-capped fury.

For Frank Wright, a deep, cleansing breath was starting to lose its magic. Hope arrived under new names now. Profiles recycled like plastic. Last night's ghost could show up tomorrow with a haunting new spell.

The next morning, still riding the faint afterglow of wine coolers and half-remembered kisses, Frank texted Nancy. He kept it casual.

> Had a great time. Would love to see you again.

Her reply came hours later.

> Me too! Just a heads-up—I'm headed to the Greek Islands with my girlfriends. Pre-planned trip. Back in two weeks... unless I marry a fisherman. :)

The smiley face landed with a thud.

By the next evening, her Instagram had become a sun-soaked mosaic of Aperol spritzes, white sand beaches, and women in coordinated linen dresses posing as if they'd just invented happiness. One shot featured what appeared to be a slow dance with a shirtless bartender named Nikos.

Frank stared at the screen, slowly released his breath, and reopened **Hearts.com**.

Swipe.

Nope.

Swipe.

Too young.

Swipe.

Is that a snake? Why is she holding a snake?

Swipe.

Face tattoo. Hard pass.

And then came Aleihs.

Platinum blonde. Every photo dipped in soft, celestial lighting, as if she traveled with her own fog machine. Her bio read as though it were a ransom note from a yoga retreat.

> "Eros is my compass. I dance barefoot to remember I'm real."

Frank squinted. He wasn't sure if she was looking for a soulmate or a podiatrist.

But it beat another night of Ron's frozen pizza and his stand-up material about fluoride and government psyops.

He swiped right.

She matched instantly.

Frank met Aleihs on a Tuesday.

The app listed her simply as *Alei.* No context, no clever quip. Just a bio that read like a set of lyrics cut from a melodramatic Taylor Swift deep track:

> Old habits die screaming. You wouldn't last an hour in the asylum where they raised me. A tortured poet. Equal parts enchantress and empath. Sushi addict. Loyal to a fault—literally. No flakes. No liars. No Leos.

Her profile was a masterclass in curated ambiguity—platinum-blonde hair cascading over one eye, silhouetted poses against dusky ocean horizons, captions rooted in the ancient practice of eros and Island girl.

Frank should've known. He should've felt it.

But something about her—her boldness, her mystery, her refusal to mention brunch or astrology apps—made her stand out, a spark in the fog. Something exotic. Maybe even mythic.

And after briefly toying with the idea of reaching out to Stefania again, he doubled down on the myth.

They agreed to meet at a quirky coffee shop near UC Berkeley—the kind of place where oat milk cost extra, tips supported a local co-op, and the baristas sometimes quoted Audre Lorde, the Black feminist poet, as they handed over your latte. Tucked just off Telegraph Avenue, the patio was dotted with mismatched chairs, well-worn tables etched with doodles and half-buried philosophies, and a rusted bike sculpture called *Oppression in Motion*.

Frank arrived early. His stomach buzzed with a mix of nerves and the remnants of a warm wine cooler he'd nursed at Ron's place while swiping through what now felt like fate.

And then she appeared.

Long blonde wig. Leopard print scarf. Black leather boots that seemed to have survived a poetry slam and a biker bar.

She moved with the kind of theatrical confidence that couldn't be faked.

"Frank," she said, her voice smoky, teasing. "You look… the same."

It took him three seconds. Recognition hit like a sucker punch to the ribs.

"Alei—wait… Sheila?"

She smiled slowly, like a cat resetting the mousetrap. "Technically, Aleihs. It's Sheila spelled backward. Reinvention's a right, you know."

Frank blinked. "We went on a date. *Weeks* ago. You said we weren't a match. You told me it would be more fun to throw rocks off Alcatraz."

She shrugged, unapologetic. "Maybe it still would be. But that was the old me."

She waved dismissively. "Come on, that was Sheila. This is Aleihs. Whole new profile. Plus, I've been in a bit of a dry spell. You seemed a better idea than another night with wine and talking to my houseplants." Frank opened his mouth. Closed it. Scanned the room for hidden cameras, a laugh track, maybe even a studio audience. Nothing. Just him.

"I figured you wouldn't remember," she went on. "Most men don't. Especially when the wig's blonde."

He tried to focus on her words, but all he could hear was Ron's voice in his head: *"You've entered the simulation, my dude. Nothing's real but the notifications."*

"So…what now?" Frank asked cautiously.

She leaned in, eyes wild with a gleam that felt half flirtation, half arrest record. "Depends. You still got that thing about your cat?"

He backed up slowly, like someone trying to defuse a glitter bomb.

"You know what, Alei—Sheila—whoever… I've got enough drama in my life." She pouted. "I thought we had chemistry."

"Are you kiddin' me?" Frank said.

"That was Shiela. Aleihs thinks you're sssexy." She said with a cat purr.

He ran out through a tangle of waiters, muttering apologies to someone he didn't bump into. Once outside, he texted Ron:

Frank: Remember the tour guide from Alcatraz?

Ron: The FBI artist or the rock-thrower?

Frank: Sure. New wig. Name's Aleihs. It's Sheila backward.

Ron: Classic! Don't bring her here, or we'll wind up with a rabbit boiling on the stove!

Frank walked on, vowing to start swiping left more aggressively—and maybe, finally, to take a break from women who spell their names with password hints.

Frank pushed open the door to Ron's apartment and was immediately hit with the sound of country music wailing at max volume. *Jolene, Jolene, Jolene, Joleeeene!*

Ron wasn't on the couch or at the table. He was flat on the carpet, eyes glassy, clutching a half-empty bag of Funyuns like morphine while Dolly Parton's voice rattled the speakers and turned the room into a honky-tonk funeral.

"Ron!" Frank shouted over the music. He went over to the stereo and twisted the volume down. "Alright, buddy—why does it sound like Dolly singing in the next room?"

Ron rolled his head toward him, eyes hollow. "Tammy Lynn."

Ron thumped his chest with Funyun-stained fingers. "She dumped me for a guy who was married to Joline. She *took Jolene's man!*"

"Wait—you're saying it's over with Tammy Lynn?" Frank asked. "So how exactly did this happen?"

Ron sat up slowly, hair wild, eyes bleak. He inhaled deeply. "The pyramid."

"The pyramid?"

Ron nodded solemnly. "I told you, amigo. The pyramid decides. I was middle tier—steady, forgettable. Tammy Lynn was climbing. Then this guy walks in already *married to a Joline* and bam! Instant celebrity tier. You don't just marry a Joline. You get enshrined in folklore."

Frank rubbed his temples. "So let me get this straight—you lost Tammy Lynn because some guy *married a Joline,* and that automatically gave him VIP access to country music celebrity?"

Ron nodded grimly. "Exactly. You can't compete with celebrity."

Frank sighed. "Well, at least you're not up against a Lucille. Then you'd have Kenny Rogers and Dolly both gunning for you."

Ron groaned. "Don't even joke, man. I can't survive that bracket."

"When did this happen?"

Ron rubbed his nose. "Right after I got your text about Sheila. Phone buzzed—Tammy Lynn. Thought it was one of those *miss you already* things." He let out a bitter laugh. "Nope. She called to say it was over… but I could keep the jars of jalapeños she'd left at my place."

Frank blinked. "She dumped you and gifted you jalapeños?"

Ron sat up. "Not just any jalapeños, my dude—heirlooms. Her grandma pickled those peppers. That's how I knew it was final: when a woman lets you keep her jalapeños, the love's gone."

Frank spotted Ron's phone on the counter, picked it up, and handed it over.

"Here," he said. "Remember—if love is rough with thou, you don't just stay on the floor."

Ron nodded, unlocked the screen, killed Spotify, and opened **HeartbreakHotel.com**—a site for people burned by a hunk of burning love.

Frank frowned. "That's real?"

Ron sighed. "You can check in anytime you like, amigo... but you can never leave."

CHAPTER 17
LIGHTS, CAMERA, OPTICS

"Don't believe what you see. If you just close your eyes, you can feel the enemy."

— **BONO**, *ACROBAT* (U2)

The kiss of the rising sun lit up the dashboard of the first-generation Prius, ushering to life the majestic Golden Gate Bridge. Below the iconic span, the wind whipped the bay waters into a white-capped fury.

For Frank Wright, a deep, cleansing breath once meant presence—boots planted on pavement, hands blackened from real fire and real work. Now it felt as though he were watching a scene from the outside. In Los Angeles, his

former life was being recast: Gail in wardrobe, Javi hitting his mark, and Mayor Apple calling the shots from behind the monitors. Truth didn't matter. The lighting was perfect. And halfway down Sunset Boulevard, innocence wasn't missing—it had been rewritten out of the script.

A modest motorcade slipped through traffic, matte-black SUVs flanked by a few camera drones hovering overhead. In the backseat of a reinforced hybrid, Mayor Apple sat cross-legged, serene and focused, her thumbs moving steadily across three screens at once.

"We'll swing by the set of *Malibu Undercover,*" she said without looking up. "You two are set to cameo as climate refugees—artisan water canteens, sandstorm goggles. Think Burning Man meets FEMA."

Gail blinked. "Climate refugees…right." The phrase lingered in the Los Angeles air, heavy as smog.

She turned toward the window, letting it all sink in. LA stretched out before her—equal parts fantasy and façade. Billboards promised new streaming hits, cosmetic fixes, and second chances. Between a dog bakery selling gluten-free biscuits and a yoga studio offering "trauma-informed stretching," Gail began to feel it.

The truth.

Maybe she had been the problem.

She had called it *a break*—a pause to evaluate, recalibrate, breathe. But now, as they moved deeper into the heart of curated unreality, she began to wonder if she'd simply pushed Frank out into the tide so she could tread water in newer, shinier pools.

Apple's voice yanked her back.

"And the *21st Century Wives of Rodeo Drive* reboot party is tonight at seven, somewhere around here," she said, swiping through notifications with the speed and flourish of a Vegas blackjack dealer.

Pixel didn't look up. "Polo Lounge. Beverly Hills Hotel."

Apple snapped her fingers. "Right—of course. Classic, iconic, oozing old-money glamour." Optics were important, and the Polo Lounge was the kind of place where avocado toast was $38 and everyone insisted they once dated Sinatra or someone's cousin who was his assistant.

Pixel offered some context to Gail. "We're updating the whole vibe—champagne waterfalls, anti-aging crystals, and a psychic who reads dating profiles instead of palms. It's feminism—just with better lighting and a stricter guest list."

Gail nodded, but her thoughts had already drifted back to Sausalito—to a man who once jump-started her dead car during finals week and made her laugh so hard she spilled an entire latte down his shirt.

She smiled at the memory, though it lingered with a quiet ache.

Javier, meanwhile, was trying to make sense of his new role in chaos. That morning, he'd offered goat milk to Apple's makeup artist. By afternoon, he was being measured for a Dodgers jersey—custom-stitched with "JAVI" across the back.

"Oh, and Javi—you're throwing out the first pitch at Dodger Stadium tomorrow," Apple said, practically glowing. "By the way, Dodger Stadium sits in Chávez Ravine — the intersection of sports heritage, community, and social justice. It's perfect. A true almost-American symbol, rising from the hills to the mound. Your story practically scripts itself." She flashed her signature grin—the kind that turned other people's lives into bullet points on a campaign slide.

Javier smiled at the mayor's makeup artist, who had turned from the front seat to flash him a grin. She held his gaze just long enough for him to not hear whatever Apple was saying.

The motorcade rolled past the faux lifeguard towers and palm tree cutouts of *Malibu Undercover's* studio lot. Everything smelled like hot pavement and ambition. A golf cart with a tinted windshield met them at the gate like a secret service escort.

Mayor Apple stepped out first, greeted by a trio of studio executives in matching linen blazers and varying degrees of hair restoration. They each said her name like they were tasting a brand they'd just invested in.

"Mayor Apple—thrilled. Thrilled. You still have that gorgeous glow about you."

Apple kissed the air beside their cheeks and adjusted her sunglasses. "You're kind to notice."

Gail barely had time to step out of the car before a clipboard-wielding assistant in bike shorts and a headset pointed her toward a trailer.

"You're Climate Refugee #2," she said. "We're thinking scorched chic. Wind damage, but sexy."

Another assistant tugged gently at Javier's arm. "You're #1. "You get dialogue. Just a few lines—all in Spanish. *Las mareas están subiendo.* The tides are rising. *Necesitamos refugio.* We need shelter. We want you to lean into the desperation. It's trauma-chic."

Gail raised an eyebrow. "Dialogue?"

"Don't worry," the assistant said, ushering them into separate dressing rooms, "we'll throw in a dirt smear and a tear stick. You both already fit the part."

The doors closed behind them with soft, hydraulic hisses.

Inside, Gail stared at the pile of distressed clothes and worn leather sandals laid out on the vanity. A name tag on the mirror read:

Refugee 2 – Gail Wright

In the next trailer, Javier was already pulling on a shredded poncho, glancing at his reflection and wondering—without wondering too hard—where the mayor's makeup artist was.

Somewhere outside, a producer shouted, "We're losing light. Let's get these tragedies lit!"

As the day unfolded, Javier spent most of the *Malibu Undercover* shoot convinced the fire was real, the screaming extras were in danger, and the golden retriever he carried from the wreckage was actually traumatized. He tried to comfort it between takes, whispering in Spanish that it was safe now. When a PA offered him trail mix and coconut water, he solemnly nodded and asked if this was part of the relief effort.

Gail watched it all with a strange detachment. The world of scripted disasters and manufactured heroism felt absurd, but then again—was it really so different from real life? Politicians hitting their marks, voters cast as background actors, crises staged for optics and applause. She almost laughed at the symmetry, though it wasn't really funny. Or maybe that was exactly why it was.

Later that night, Javier was clean-shaven, cologned, and seated at the Polo Lounge.

The iconic landmark oozed with ritz—leather banquettes, pink tablecloths, and waiters who poured champagne with the precision of Olympic athletes. Studio power brokers mingled with reality stars and cosmetic dentists, all pretending they weren't watching the room while absolutely watching the room.

Near the grand piano, a flatscreen ran a looped teaser from *Hollywood Stories*—a nightly tabloid show that packaged celebrity into bite-sized scandal.

Tonight's top headline:

> "CLIMATE COUPLE? THE MAYOR, THE EX-WIFE, AND HER NEW FLAME—INSIDE THE LUXE LIFE OF A POLITICAL LOVE STORY."

Gail sat beneath a framed black-and-white photo of a younger Sinatra holding court, her dress tasteful, her posture politely indifferent. Guests leaned in, eager for proximity and a quote.

"So... did you meet on an app or, like, in the wild?"

"Is he Hollywood-famous, or just Instagram-famous?"

"Would you consider launching a couples' podcast—something healing but edgy?"

She smiled, gave them what they came for. Something about change. Something about strength. Across the room, Javier lingered near a glowing champagne tower that pulsed like a high-end jukebox. Somewhere between his third cocktail and a bite of pâté served on a crouton that inexplicably tasted like warm plantains, he gave up trying to make sense of the questions. People circled him like sharks that had scented fresh blood in designer cologne.

None of it real.

"So... do you still do the firefighter stuff?"

"Do you get scared?"

"What's your favorite part—hoses or parties?"

Javier smiled, nodded, took another sip. Whatever they thought he was, it apparently came with free drinks.

He handed out the "3E" shirts Pixel had given him earlier.

"Sí... es buen trabajo," he said, then paused, searching for the words. "Is... good job. Sometimes... fuego muy grande. Big fire, yes."

Someone chuckled—not at him, but at the effort. Sincere, stumbling, and somehow more honest than anything else in the room.

Another guest asked, "What's the most intense call you've responded to?"

Nearby, Pixel translated the question into Spanish with mechanical precision. Javier thought for a moment, then shrugged.

"Una vez… gato en árbol. Muy alto." He lifted his hand to show how high, then added with a grin, "One time… cat. In tree. Very… very up."

He grabbed a flute of champagne from a passing tray and raised it proudly.

"¡Por el gato! To cat!"

Laughter rippled around him. He still wasn't sure what half the questions meant—but the lights were warm, the drinks were free, and everyone seemed to love him. For now, that was enough.

As Gail moved through the room, a woman with perfect cheekbones and an insincere smile touched her elbow.

"You have such a beautiful stillness," she said. "You and Javi? You're the story America didn't know it needed. Renewal, without the mess."

Gail gave a look that passed for gratitude.

"Yeah," she said. "We try to keep it tidy."

As the night wound down and faux celebrities slipped out the side doors, no camera ever caught a real moment between Gail and Javier—because none existed. The whispers, the staged warmth—it was all performance. They had never shared a bed, only a storyline. Javier still slept in Frank's old mancave in Sausalito—on a futon, under a faded Joe Montana poster, beside a fireman's axe no one touched anymore. It wasn't a tool now, only a relic—kept as a memory of what used to matter.

She let him move in because he needed help. Helping made her feel useful—like someone who did the right thing, even when it wasn't right for her. And it didn't hurt that the mayor was sending direct deposit payments to her account on Javier's behalf.

She told herself it was kindness. Compassion. But sometimes, in the middle of the night when the house was still and the only sound was TC's paws on the hardwood floor, she wondered if it was just easier than facing the silence Frank left behind.

The truth, of course, was quieter than any of the narratives Pixel had polished and Apple had rehearsed. Despite the storyline of new beginnings and post-marriage passion, Gail and Javier had not consummated anything. Not in the way people assumed.

She wasn't in love with Javier—wasn't even sure she liked him. But compassion had become her reflex, a trait others admired, the kind that opened doors and drew applause. After Frank left, admiration wasn't just pleasant—it was currency. Safe. Steady. Like a paycheck—

a direct-deposit paycheck, courtesy of the mayor.

Someone handed her another drink as a woman from a streaming platform with a voice thick and syrupy cornered her.

"Do you think standing beside Javi helps the mayor—or helps you?" she asked, almost sweetly.

Gail forced a smile. "That's the question, isn't it?"

Across the lounge, the mayor stood radiant under a barrage of camera flashes, spinning phrases like "ethical rebirth" and "post-truth unity" with champagne in one hand and a crowd of sycophants in the other.

Pixel leaned in just behind her, phone aglow. "You're up three points in the polls, Mayor. Among likely viewers and registered voters."

Apple didn't blink. "Of course I am," she said, raising her glass high for the next flash.

Near the entrance, Javi caught the eye of the mayor's makeup artist again. She gave him a look Gail never had—not tidy, not rehearsed, not polished for a photo op. It was messy. Warm. Seductive.

The kind of look that said *I see you,*

Not *I need you to scoop TC's litter box.*

CHAPTER 18

TITANIC THOUGHTS

"And you may tell yourself, 'This is not my beautiful house… This is not my beautiful wife.'"

— **TALKING HEADS,** *ONCE IN A LIFETIME*

The kiss of the rising sun lit up the dashboard of the first-generation Prius, ushering to life the majestic Golden Gate Bridge. Below the iconic span, the wind whipped the bay waters into a white-capped fury.

For Frank Wright, a deep, cleansing breath failed to stop the slow rise of dread. He wasn't drowning—but he wasn't treading water either. Just floating, emotionally hypoxic.

The likes had dried up. The follows slowed. Whatever digital stardust Frank had kicked up from his brief flirtation with viral fame had long since settled into algorithmic sediment.

His phone, once a hotbox of buzz and flirtatious emojis, now buzzed for app updates and Ron's "emergency" messages about new material.

Nancy was still in Greece. She sent the occasional text—two days late, timestamped in weird afternoon hours like she was answering from a sun-soaked veranda in a different life.

Frank told himself it was fine. Romantic purgatory with scenic backdrops still beat rejection.

It was during a Tuesday fire safety class at the rec center—half PowerPoint, half CPR puppet show—that Frank got caught swiping. He thought he was being subtle.

He wasn't.

"You ever try looking up instead of down?" a voice said.

Frank looked up. Across the desk, a wiry man in his early sixties studied him—vintage denim jacket, a face weathered and familiar, the look of a conman past his prime.

"Been swiping since '03," the man said, cracking his knuckles. "Before apps, there were forums. Before that? Classified ads. Hell, I was even a contestant on *Love Connection.* Cupid just keeps changing the font—two and two, forever."

Frank laughed, not catching the Chuck Woolery reference. A little embarrassed, he asked, "You get any better at it?"

The man snorted. "You don't get better. You get... fluent. There's a difference."

His name was Jesse Coltrain. Lived alone, drove a hybrid, took ballroom dancing classes on Thursdays, and had what he called "the full collector's set of romantic disappointment."

"The truth is," Jesse said, looking around, "everyone's got baggage at this point. It's not about whether they do—it's about whether they're still pretending they don't."

He sipped from a dented Raiders tumbler. "And women? At my age, they don't really need us—not like before. They've got their dance groups, retirement hobbies, grandkids, Netflix queues. More than half have money—either from a divorce or a dead husband. And the ones not stuck in the fog of menopause? They've got a better relationship with the friend in their nightstand drawer than with any guy who shows up late and forgets to text back." Frank blinked, caught off guard.

He wasn't sure whether to laugh or be scared.

Jesse didn't sound bitter—just seasoned, someone who'd been through the storm and returned with the weather report.

"I went on a date last week," Jesse continued. "She asked me if I had any red flags. Told her I'd been married three times."

Frank winced.

Jesse grinned. "She told me that was a red flag. I told her no, sweetheart, a red flag would've been if I told the truth—four times."

They both laughed. Loud enough for the CPR students to look up from their workbooks.

Frank studied Jesse's wiry frame, the denim jacket with frayed cuffs, the practiced ease of a man who'd long since stopped pretending at optimism. *Was that what waited for him?*

"So, what keeps you going?" Frank asked. "I mean… after the fourth, don't you just hang it up?"

Jesse shook his head, amused at the naïveté.

"Kid, hanging it up is the illusion. You think I'm chasing love? Nah. I'm chasing conversation, a spark, a reason to shave in the morning. The apps, the meetups, the 'let's grab coffee' charades—it's all just proof you're still in the game."

Frank leaned forward.

"And does it work?"

Jesse's grin softened into something almost kind.

"Sometimes. Most nights it's a strikeout. But every once in a while, you get a hit—a laugh that sticks, a night you remember. That's enough. Doesn't have to be forever. Forever's a young man's delusion."

Frank felt the words settle heavier than he expected. He wasn't sure if Jesse was warning him or handing him a map.

Later, as Frank walked to his car, Jesse's words clung to him heavier than any of Ron's caffeinated soundbites. There was something oddly comforting in the honesty—like being told the bad news by someone who knew how to survive it.

Frank didn't know what came next. But for the first time in a while, he didn't feel as if he was the only one out of sync with the dance.

Back at Ron's loft, Frank sat on the edge of the futon with a half-finished wine cooler and his phone glowing at 12% battery.

The place was quiet for once—no Texas bowling queens, no axe-throwing drills, just the faint hum of traffic and Ron muttering comic bombs in the shower.

Jesse's voice echoed in his head: *"It's not about whether they've got baggage. It's whether they're still pretending they don't."*

Frank opened his dating app, stared at his profile photo—him on a kayak from five years and fifteen pounds ago—and tapped "Edit."

He started typing, slower than usual, this time without Ron

hovering over his shoulder, pitching slogans like *"Emotionally available and grilled cheese-capable."*

> Frank, 41
>
> 📍 San Francisco • 6'1" • Still learning
>
> Former firefighter. Once ran into burning buildings—now just trying to walk into good conversations.
>
> Not here for games, unless it's trivia night or figuring out which streaming service we both forgot to cancel.
>
> Been married. Been wrong. Still believe in right.
>
> I've got a cat who judges everyone and a best friend who swears axe-throwing is therapy.
>
> Not pretending I don't have a past—I do. But I'm not dragging it behind me in a broken suitcase.
>
> I cook. I clean (most of the time). And yes, I know the good olive oil.
>
> Swipe right if you're done chasing fairy tales and ready for something real—awkward pauses, midnight snacks, and late-night honesty included.

As his thumb hovered over "Save," a flicker of memory surfaced—one of those small, quiet ones that never fully left.

He and Gail, sitting on the couch in Sausalito, trying to book a weekend cabin. She read every Yelp review out loud like it was gospel, annotating them with commentary and laughter.

"These people say the walls are too thin," she'd said, mock whispering. *"Let's go test that theory."*

Back then, her voice had felt like guidance. Now, the silence felt louder than ever.

Frank stared at the final sentence for a long moment, then smiled—small, tired, but genuine—and tapped it.

Profile updated.

One last thing Jesse had said after class drifted back to Frank—slow, deliberate, like it had been left behind on purpose:

"Online dating isn't about finding the right person—it's about picking your favorite deck chair while the Titanic goes down, and deciding which part of the ship you're willing to sink with."

Cynical, yet oddly refreshing. Maybe the problem had been all the auditioning, the constant performance. Just showing up—perhaps that was the answer. And maybe, just maybe, it was enough. It was the advice he hadn't known he needed.

CHAPTER 19
WILD PITCH

"In politics, absurdity is not a handicap."

— NAPOLEON BONAPARTE

The kiss of the rising sun lit up the dashboard of the first-generation Prius, ushering to life the majestic Golden Gate Bridge. Below the iconic span, the wind whipped the bay waters into a white-capped fury.

For Frank Wright, a deep, cleansing breath wasn't just ritual—it was renewal. Something had shifted. The kind of shift that doesn't come with fanfare, just the quiet click of a door opening that had stayed shut too long. Whatever was coming next, he wasn't bracing for it. He was stepping into it.

Javier threw out the first pitch at the Dodgers game—sort of. The ball skipped once, bounced twice, and rolled gently into the catcher's mitt, similar to a putt on the ninth green. Still, the crowd cheered, Mayor Apple clapped, and somewhere in the stadium, a camera caught the moment just right—making it appear like a triumph rather than political comedy.

By the seventh inning, Javier was last seen double-fisting a Dodger Dog and a tallboy of Modelo, grinning as if freshly smitten—someone who'd just fallen for a makeup artist who knew that football didn't mean soccer. He never made it to the owner's suite, where Mayor Apple and the mayor of Los Angeles were waiting—cameras primed, smiles loaded, the symbolism already prepackaged.

Outside, the limo idled at the VIP entrance. Inside, Gail and Pixel sat—poised, polished, and waiting. No Javier. No makeup artist. Just the hum of the engine and the slow, shared realization that whatever this had been... was booting grounders it couldn't afford.

By morning, he was simply gone. No updates, no sightings, not even a rumor. Just an empty seat in the limo and a lot of unanswered texts. Stadium cameras caught Javier and his female friend leaving the concourse behind home plate and blending into a crowd before disappearing entirely.

The neat little narrative the mayor's office had been feeding the public was coming apart like a knockoff handbag at the zipper.

Seventy-two hours. No Javier. No leads. No plan B.

The campaign suite had shifted from organized chaos to political freefall. Mayor Apple's phone pinged every ten seconds. Her inbox was a landfill of urgency. The calendar was stacked with high-visibility appearances—union breakfasts, eco-summits, a digital town hall with influencers who spoke only in filters and acronyms. The schedule wasn't just busy; it was merciless. Panic was no longer whispered. It was on payroll.

"We need something now!" Mayor Apple snapped, sweeping aside a stack of mock-up posters. "Donors are calling. Press is circling. We can't cancel again without blood in the water."

Pixel, perched on the edge of the conference table with a latte in hand and the focused expression of someone calculating political odds in real time, offered a long shot.

"I have one idea. It's extreme."

Apple spun toward her. "Please. At this point, I'd consider a Javier hologram."

Pixel didn't blink. "Frank Wright."

Silence.

The mayor was stunned, like she'd just been asked to bring back the flip phone. "What?! Firefighter Frank Wright? You want to replace Javier—who replaced Frank Wright—with Frank Wright?"

Pixel didn't flinch. "Yes. It's ironic. But it's workable. I mean, they already look alike—same build, same jawline, same hair thing going on. He's Javier, but more pale."

Apple stared at her for a long beat, then let out a slow breath through her nose. "So let me get this straight—you want to solve the disappearing immigrant boyfriend problem by slapping a fresh coat of Latino gloss on the original husband?"

Pixel stepped closer, calm and unshaken. "Mayor, at this point if the story's broken, sometimes you've got to reboot the pilot with a familiar face and less lighting."

Apple didn't respond. She turned on her heel and walked straight toward Gail, who sat quietly scrolling through an endless thread of unanswered texts.

"Gail," the mayor said, voice smooth but steely. "I have a proposal. We need Frank to step in—as Javier. Just for appearances. A few photo ops, some hand-holding. Until we locate our favorite Honduran Houdini, it's optics over authenticity."

Gail looked up, shocked. "You want Frank to impersonate Javier?"

"Briefly," Apple said, already spinning it in her mind. "Strategically. We blur a few lines, soften the lighting, and keep the narrative intact. You think voters notice? Half of them think Elvis is alive and working at a Cracker Barrel in Fresno."

Gail blinked. "That's insane."

Apple smiled. "It's not insane. It's politics."

"I haven't spoken to Frank since he left," Gail said. "He wouldn't pick up if I were on fire."

"Then give him something to come back for," Apple said coolly. "Tell him we'll give him his old job back. Full reinstatement. No hoops, no press, no fine print. All he has to do is pretend to be the man who replaced him… long enough to save the campaign."

Gail looked at the mayor like she had just asked her to eat glass.

But Apple simply smiled, unbothered.

"Call it poetic. Call it political. Call it whatever you want—just make the call."

Gail didn't respond right away. She just stared at the mayor, knowing full well what this was. Not a suggestion. A directive wrapped in charm.

By the time she stepped outside, the sun had started to dip behind the hills—and her thumb hovered over Frank's contact, the screen glowing like it knew better.

Back at Ron's loft, Frank lay half-reclined on a couch that had the spinal support of a beach towel. A muted true crime documentary flickered across the TV, casting erratic flashes of blue and red over mismatched furniture and a half-eaten bag of pretzels. Outside, a neon sign for *Cloud Command Vape* buzzed with the urgency of a dying mosquito.

His phone pinged on the coffee table.

TEXT FROM GAIL:

> Hey. Hope you're doing okay. Sorry, I've been in a bad place.

Frank glanced at it and froze. Anxiety punched him square in the gut. He didn't answer.

Ping.

TEXT FROM GAIL:

> Random question—do you still have your old city windbreaker?

He picked up the phone, typed *Why?*—then deleted it. He set the phone back down, this time face down.

Ping.

TEXT FROM GAIL:

> Please, Frank. I just need to talk. Just for a second.

Frank scoffed. He stood, walked over to the tiny fridge, cracked open a wine cooler, and took a long gulp.

"Seven months of silence," he muttered, "and now she needs wardrobe inventory?"

He drank again, slower this time. The carbonation stung at the corners of his mouth. Outside the loft window, dusk drifted between the buildings, withdrawing like someone quietly leaving the room—taking with it the last traces of warmth they once shared.

He sat up. His phone buzzed again on the coffee table. Face down. Still glowing.

> I don't blame you for not wanting to talk,
> but this is especially important.

He stared at the message. The wine cooler warmed in his hand.

Eighteen years. That wasn't just history—it was muscle memory. A second language spoken in shared routines and quiet shorthand. He could still hear her rhythms, feel her essence in the small, unthinking gestures that had once defined their relationship—

and now it was gone. And yet here he was, pacing in a borrowed loft above a vape shop, being asked if he still had his old city-issued windbreaker.

As if that was all that remained of him.

He rubbed his eyes, let out a breath he didn't realize he'd been holding.

Had there been signs? Maybe—the small fires Gail hinted at, the kind that smolder in silence. But Frank only knew the real kind, the ones that filled a room with smoke and demanded water, not reflection.

There was a time when Gail used to leave handwritten notes in his lunch—just dumb stuff, jokes, little affirmations. Those had stopped around the time fertility doctor visits became monthly calendars, hormone panels, and quiet car rides home. When hope turned clinical, and each cycle felt closer to a countdown than a beginning.

Not long after, she read *The Myth of Us*, a book that left her wondering if some futures were simply illusions. Motherhood, the family she'd pictured—it all slipped further away with every failed attempt. The guest room became a hollow space, carefully emptied of reminders: no crib, no toys, just stacked boxes and a silence that thickened by the day. She moved through those days dulled and unfinished, her sentences trailing into nothing. It was as if she were already slipping out the door long before she closed it.

Still, he hadn't seen it coming. Not really. Because Frank had read somewhere—maybe in an article, maybe just a quote—that women often define love through presence, while men express it through actions. And he believed—truly believed—that showing up, fixing what was broken, and carrying the weight day after day was what counted.

He'd carried the groceries. Paid the bills. Showed up when the cat got sick. Fixed the dryer. He thought that was love.

But maybe that was the problem.

Do men fall apart when they lose purpose?

Or do women simply outgrow the men who keep mistaking duty for depth?

Frank thought, *Was I her constant... or just the one who stayed put?* He felt foolish. Not just for believing it would last—but for believing that love didn't need to change if it was built on something solid.

She wanted growth. Expansion. Forward motion.

And he? He just wanted things to stop breaking.

Now, she was asking to talk. Probably not to rekindle—just to get something from him.

He picked up the phone. Typed:

Why.

Deleted it.

Typed:

Now you want to talk?

Deleted that, too.

He placed the phone back down, this time gently. As if it would explode.

The strange thing was, he wasn't angry. Not anymore. He wasn't even sad.

He was just... tired.

Because whoever she was now, she wasn't *his* Gail. She was a stranger in a familiar body, asking him a silly question in text form.

He took another sip, leaned back, and stared up at the cracked ceiling.

Eighteen years, he thought.

And this is what's left. A borrowed couch, a wine cooler, and a text that reads like a summons.

Outside traffic hummed.

For the first time in months, his silence felt like clarity. He took another drink.

CHAPTER 20

THE CRISIS OF EROS

The worst part of holding the memories is not the pain. It's the loneliness of it."

— **LOIS LOWRY,** *THE GIVER*

The kiss of the rising sun lit up the dashboard of the first-generation Prius, ushering to life the majestic Golden Gate Bridge. Below the iconic span, the wind whipped the bay waters into a white-capped fury.

For Frank Wright, a deep, cleansing breath still came each morning, though he no longer knew what it cleared. Time passed. Messages sat unread. Familiar names reappeared in unfamiliar ways. Nothing had broken. Not all

at once. But some things don't crack—they just fade until someone notices the silence.

Gail stepped into Firehouse 11, her heels clicking softly against the concrete floor as memories washed over her. She could still picture the old days—surprise visits with baskets of muffins, Frank grinning at her from across the truck bay, the crew teasing him as brothers would around a campfire. Back when the station smelled of smoke and soap and carried the weight of family. Now, it felt off—familiar, but drained, the warmth replaced by echoes.

A few crew members offered polite hellos. Most just watched her pass with quiet curiosity.

She found her way to the lockers and leaned against them, gripping her phone as if it weighed a hundred pounds.

Across from her, perched on a low folding bench as if it had been built just for him, sat Jax Brown—better known around Station 11 (and half of Northern California) as Micro Jax. Before the helmet and turnout gear, he'd been a pro on the micro-wrestling circuit, infamous for his bouts with Half Nelson. In the department, he earned a reputation as an arson whisperer, the guy who could sniff accelerant through drywall and talk a blaze down like it owed him money.

Now semi-retired, he lived in the gray space between firefighter, prank legend, and certified chaos goblin. Small frame, oversized presence—all heart. For years, Jax had been Frank's closest firehouse buddy, his partner in both emergencies and bad decisions.

"I've sent repeated texts," Gail said, her voice flat. "He's not answering."

Jax didn't look surprised. "Yeah, well… can you blame him? You didn't just break his heart—you bulldozed his life."

She blinked but didn't look away.

"Men like Frank?" Jax continued, running his hand across his balding head. "They don't come home for comfort unless they've got something out there that makes 'em feel like somebody. That job? That was his compass. You rip that out, and you don't just get a confused man—you get a wounded one. And when home turns cold on top of that?" He shrugged. "All he's got left is a cat that won't listen, reruns of *Springer*, and just enough time to wonder where it all went sideways."

Gail exhaled slowly, her composure slipping.

"I panicked, Jax. Everything changed so fast. Frank wasn't Frank anymore—he was angry, distant, spiraling. And I didn't know anymore."

She rubbed her hands.

"Then came your barbecue… and not long after, the mayor called. One pitch turned into another, and suddenly I was swept into this swirl of optics and inclusion. And then—there's Javier. Standing in my kitchen. Wearing Frank's old fire-resistant boots like he was some kind of stand-in. A placeholder for a version of my life I hadn't processed losing."

She laughed, but it faltered almost immediately. "The boots didn't even fit. They flopped when he walked. But weirdly, that made it easier to pretend everything wasn't collapsing. It felt like theater—as if I just kept hitting my cues, the script would make sense. One moment I was trying to salvage a life with Frank, and the next, I was being staged for a press conference next to someone who barely spoke English... but carried the kind of progress people could root for."

Her voice lowered.

"I wasn't trying to replace Frank. I was just trying to survive the silence."

Jax leaned forward, elbows on his knees, and gave her a look that felt heavier than his small frame.

"So now you want Frank to do what?" he asked. "Just move on like nothing happened?"

"No," Gail said quietly. "I just want to give him the chance to decide if he wants to fix it—on his own terms."

Jax sat with that. Then nodded.

"Well, that's progress," he said. "Painful, late-stage progress. But progress."

He stood, stretched, and cracked his neck as if he was about to suit up for a high-rise rescue.

Jax nodded. "I'll talk to him. He'll listen—or fake it just enough to keep from throwing me out the window."

He started toward the bay doors and turned mid-step.

"I'll be honest, this feels like stepping back into the ring as the heel—getting booed by the crowd, wearing a plastic championship belt, and trying to sell him on an emotional comeback right after hitting him with a folding chair to the skull."

"Jax," Gail said quietly.

He noticed a strain in her voice.

"There's one more thing," she said. "I want to be transparent with you—I don't want to hide anything."

Jax narrowed his eyes, lips pressed tight. Suspicious.

"Javi left," she said. "During the Dodgers game. Just got up and vanished—no one's seen him since."

Jax stared, mouth slightly open, trying to process.

"The mayor wants Frank to step in. Pretend to be Javi. Just for two weeks. Campaign trail stuff. Photos, appearances, baby-kissing. If he does it... she's offering him his old job back. Full benefits. All his severance time."

Jax staggered backward as if struck, the shock landing like a psychological slap. He reached for the bench—and missed completely. A moment later, he hit the floor with a solid thud.

"What?!" he barked. "Are you serious?"

"Please, Jax," Gail said. "It would be good for everyone."

Still on the floor, Jax let out a groan and rolled his eyes toward the ceiling. "That's not a plan—that's a deleted scene from a telenovela... or the opening round of a Royal Rumble. Either way, someone's getting slapped."

Shaking his head, Jax saw it clearly. "Classic Eve. She'll stoop to anything to get what she wants. Trust me, I've got the scars."

He hauled himself up, brushing off his cargo pants like he'd just gone three rounds with a moral dilemma.

"Alright," he said. "I'll tell him. But convincing a guy who got dumped and replaced to play dress-up for the people who tossed him under the bus? That's a tall order—even for me."

Two hours later, across town, a knock echoed off the metal stairs. Frank opened the door to find Jax—holding a six-pack of Modelo and a folded firehouse T-shirt.

"Jax! What are you doing here?" Frank asked.

"Just checking in—seeing how rock bottom's treating you."

Frank stepped aside. Jax walked in and eyed the loft: the sagging futon, Ron's pictures of Tammy Lynn bowling covering every available inch of wall space, and a suspicious pile of empty wine cooler boxes near the kitchen.

"Place smells like pickled regret," Jax said.

"Yeah, Ron's into bowling and jalapeño-laced foods these days," Frank replied.

Jax tossed Frank a cold one, then plopped onto the beanbag chair that groaned under protest.

"Patty tried to toast a bagel in the hazmat gear dryer—thought the thing worked like a convection oven. Set off the ammonia alarm. We had to evacuate two Girl Scout troops, and poor old Blue nearly found the bone yard."

Frank laughed, then went quiet.

"So, is this a social call, or is there something else?" he asked.

"I brought beer, so yeah—it's friendly. But there's more." Jax paused. "It's about Gail. And before you chuck a bottle, just listen. She reached out. Said she needs to talk. Said it's important. Now, I'm not saying she deserves consideration or a do-over, but she didn't sound like someone playing games. And if anyone's gonna run into this burning building without getting burned, it's me."

Frank shook his head. "Jax, it's been seven months. Seven long months. I mean long! If this was so important, she could've said so before the cryptic texts and the sudden windbreaker nostalgia."

"Windbreakers?" Jax snorted, struggling to sit upright on the chair that swallowed people whole. "Frank, this is big."

He leaned in, eyes wide. "There's a problem in the mayor's campaign—something serious—and word is, she's scrambling for a fix."

He paused, letting the sentence hang in the air.

"She's got a proposal. One that could put you back in your old boots. Full benefits. Back pay. The whole damn nine."

Frank narrowed his eyes. "What are you saying?"

"I'm saying it's a mess. A political one," Jax said. "Javi vanished. Gail's caught in the crossfire, and the mayor's media tour is going up in smoke."

Frank took a long drink, trying to connect the dots. "So... what do they want with me?"

"They want you to step in. Pretend to be Javier—for a couple of weeks. Smile for the cameras, shake hands, play the role. In return? You get your job back. Full benefits. Back pay. Clean slate."

Frank dropped his full weight beside Jax, the impact jolted Jax clear off the vinyl chair, sending him up in the air before crashing down on top of Frank. For a moment, Frank's face went pale, eyes glassy and distant, as if he'd just taken a punch he didn't see coming. The impact of it—everything—was settling in.

"I'm sorry, brother," Jax said gently. "This whole thing is pro wrestling—just with more lies and better costumes."

Frank leaned forward, elbows on his knees, the Modelo bottle dangling between his fingers. The sunlight from the loft window stretched across the room, a spotlight catching the worn edges of his old firehouse T-shirt still folded on the table.

"You know what the worst part is?" he said quietly. "It's not the pretending. I mean, I've been pretending since the day I got terminated. Pretending I'm fine. Pretending I'm over it. Pretending I no longer love Gail."

Jax said nothing, just listened, the way only someone who'd been through their own firestorms could.

Frank stood, pacing now, bottle in hand, eyes flicking between the cluttered chaos of Ron's place and the world beyond the windows.

"This gig—they're handing me my old life like it's a leftover casserole. Reheated. Repackaged. But it's not mine anymore."

He stopped near the window and stared outside.

"My boots? Some guy with no last name is wearing them. My house? Feels more like a museum I used to live in than a home. And Gail…"

He hesitated.

"She gave up too fast. Way too fast. What happened to 'til death do us part'? Guess that part just expires when the optics aren't convenient."

He could see the blurry lights of Sausalito across the bay. "But if I say no, what am I holding on to? Pride? Principle? I've got a futon, a cat who doesn't live with me, and a best friend who hosts open mics at a bowling alley."

Jax stood and moved beside him. "You want your life back, Frank. I get it. But not at the cost of pretending to be the dude that replaced you."

Frank exhaled, compromise pressing down on him. He looked at the T-shirt, then at the chair, and finally at Jax. "I just don't know if I'm saving something… or burying it."

Jax gave him a long look and said softly, "Sometimes, brother, it's both."

CHAPTER 21

BRING OUT THE CLOWNS

"Compromise makes a good umbrella but a poor roof."

—JAMES RUSSELL LOWELL

The kiss of the rising sun lit up the dashboard of the first-generation Prius, ushering to life the majestic Golden Gate Bridge. Below the iconic span, the wind whipped the bay waters into a white-capped fury.

For Frank Wright, a deep, cleansing breath once meant order—do the job, follow the steps, no mayor holding a photo op.

City Hall smelled of old ambition and lemon disinfectant. Frank followed Ron through the marble lobby, past security, and up the grand staircase that led to the mayor's suite of offices. Along the hallway, glossy handshake photos lined the walls—Mayor Apple grinning beside U.S. presidents, prime ministers, tech billionaires, notable clergy, and at least one man who looked suspiciously like the rapper Bullpit.

Frank tugged at the collar of his only collared shirt—Ron had insisted he wear it "to signal readiness to negotiate." His Topsiders squeaked against the pristine floor, as if even his shoes knew he didn't belong.

They entered the mayor's office.

"Frank Wright! There he is!" Pixel said, flashing a too-bright smile as she crossed the room, tablet tucked under her arm. She beamed as though Frank were a long-lost cousin instead of a last-ditch effort to save the mayor from a political blunder.

Mayor Apple stood beside her, arms open in welcome, pantsuit so crisp it looked sharp enough to slice bread.

"Frank! So thrilled to see you. You look… well!" the mayor said, voice high with strategic cheer.

"Thanks. I… yeah, thanks," Frank replied, stepping cautiously into the office.

Pixel and the mayor traded glossy, politician-grade smiles, as if the last seven months of silence, scandal, and scapegoating were nothing more than a clerical error. The air was polite, rehearsed, and unmistakably fake.

Frank gestured to the man beside him.

"This is Ron. He's my… representative. Also, my close friend and advisor."

Ron stepped forward with a grin. "Pleasure. I'll be assisting Mr. Wright in these negotiations. Full disclosure—I did pass the LSAT, so let's keep the legal gymnastics to a minimum."

He delivered the line with the confidence of a man who hadn't read a contract in years but still somehow understood leverage. Unshaven, hair askew, and wearing a slightly wrinkled tuxedo jacket over a vintage *Free Britney* T-shirt, Ron looked like a groomsman who'd taken a wrong turn at a beach wedding and ended up negotiating a hostage release at City Hall.

Pixel nodded smoothly. "Of course. We're thinking minimal lift, high impact. Frank steps in for Javier—press stops, photo ops, maybe a ribbon-cutting or two. It's a simple visual continuity play."

Mayor Apple stepped closer. "Think of it as… a soft reboot. Same face, lighter tan, slightly different accent."

Frank blinked. "So, I'm… impersonating the guy who replaced me?"

"Technically, yes," Pixel said, her gaze steady. "Symbolically, you're stepping into the outline of municipal diversity. Two weeks. In and out. We'll manage the rest."

Mayor Apple chimed in, her tone slick and deliberate. "And in return—your old position. Full benefits. Back pay. Clean slate."

Frank blinked and nodded in unbelief. Ron leaned in.

"Also, we'll need 49ers tickets in the mayor's suite—nothing fancy, just a soft seat somewhere between the donors and the retired linebackers—and a monthly case of wine coolers, imported from France, preferably. Frank insists on drinking like it's prom night, 1987. Same playlist, too."

Mayor Apple didn't flinch. "You'll get two nosebleed seats—section 342, row Z. A voucher for two domestic beers and one salted pretzel per game." She glanced at her aide. "No substitutions."

She turned to Ron: "Imported wine coolers? This isn't Versailles."

Frank shifted in his chair, still unsure if this was a dream, a scam, or some twisted civic improv skit.

"You people are unbelievable," he said.

Mayor Apple leaned forward, her smile tight and her tone colder now. "Wake up, Frank. You're not some wide-eyed rookie—we both know that. This is the underbelly of the real world. Optics, deals, leverage. You want justice? Try a movie."

She paused just long enough for the words to land. "This is the best offer you're going to get to recover your pathetic little life. Take it… or keep sulking above a vape shop."

Frank's eyes narrowed. "I want a direct apology. From you, Mayor. No sidestepping, no 'miscommunications.' You wrecked my life. I want to hear you own that."

The mayor exhaled slowly, then gave a shallow nod. "You'll get your apology—privately. No cameras, no press release. Just words. That's all I can offer."

Her voice sharpened. "But in return, I want your silence. Absolute discretion. You'll sign a non-disclosure agreement and a statement of full confidentiality. This arrangement doesn't leave this room, doesn't go to the press, doesn't become pillow talk or podcast material. Understood?"

"I don't do podcasts," Frank said.

Ron lifted a hand. "But we're open to offers."

Frank turned toward the walls, scanning more handshake photos—smiles frozen in history, deals inked in exchange for something invisible. Trade what's left of my dignity for two weeks? Or keep sipping wine coolers above a vape shop?

Two weeks.

He exhaled.

Ten minutes later, the deal was done.

Now Frank sat under the blinding vanity lights of a makeshift dressing room inside City Hall, flanked by two

Hollywood makeup artists blending, bronzing, and contouring as if prepping him for the Oscars. A wardrobe specialist with a headset and attitude adjusted the buttons on his pressed firehouse uniform—Javier's uniform, tailored for someone just a bit leaner and much more photogenic.

On the far end of the room, a wiry man in a guayabera stood with arms folded. He spoke in a rich Honduran accent, eyes scanning Frank the way a sculptor studies a lump of clay.

"Again, from the diaphragm—'La comunidad está en buenas manos.' You must feel the words, not just say them."

"Can I feel them in my own voice?" Frank asked.

"Only if your voice is from Honduras."

Meanwhile, Pixel paced in the corner, cue cards fanned in her trembling hands, editing each line as if it were a rung on the ladder she'd been climbing for years. Every word mattered. This wasn't just spin—it was survival. One slip, and she'd tumble back into the pool of nameless interns; nail it, and she'd stand one step closer to the podium herself.

Mayor Apple burst in with a trail of staff, all armed with tablets, ring lights, and iced matcha lattes.

"Alright, team—Shake House in 90 minutes," she announced. "We're shaking up California for everybody, not just the ones with trust funds and lobbyist connections. I want energy, unity, visible diversity, without visible pores.

This is the road to smart cities, people—let's sell it." She turned to Frank.

"You look great. A little more... Latin, which is the point. But not too Latin. Vague enough to photograph well. That's the sweet spot."

Frank didn't respond. He just tugged at his new collar and tried not to hyperventilate.

Pixel's earpiece buzzed.

Pixel leaned in through the side door, her voice crisp and clinical. "Gail's here. She's waiting in the green room."

Frank froze. Seven months of silence collapsed into a single, immediate inhale.

Of course, she was here. The one person he hadn't rehearsed for.

He felt something tighten in his chest—not anger exactly, and not grief either. Just that moment when the air itself seems to tighten around you.

For a second, he wondered if he'd turn around, walk out, let everyone figure it out without him.

But he didn't.

Now, Frank stepped through the curtain.

Tan, trimmed, and stiff in Javier's tailored firehouse uniform, he looked like the uncanny valley version of himself—familiar but off. The cologne they'd sprayed him with lingered in the air, citrusy and foreign. Every movement felt like it belonged to someone else.

Gail stood near the mirror, hands folded in front of her, wearing a teal blazer the campaign stylist called "Shallow Water." Her expression was of someone who had practiced this moment but couldn't remember which version she'd rehearsed. To Mayor Apple, she was the new face of the modern woman—poised but approachable, stylish without excess, a survivor polished into a brand. The kind of figure who could stand beside a candidate and silently sell resilience, progress, reinvention. Gail, though, wasn't sure if she was playing a part or disappearing into one. She smiled when she saw him.

"Wow," she said softly. "They really leaned into the makeover, huh?"

Frank gave a half-smile. "I barely recognize myself. But hey, the accent coach stopped short of tattooing Latin Kings on my back. So, there's that."

They stood there, not quite close enough to touch, but too close for small talk to feel safe.

"I didn't know how to initiate anything," Gail said, her voice cautious. "Then it felt too late… and then it all turned into politics."

"Yeah." Frank's eyes drifted to the corner, where campaign staffers were buzzing around with clipboards and cables like caffeinated stagehands. "It's fine. Just another chapter in the world's weirdest memoir. I mean, why watch *Jerry*

Springer when you can be the unwitting guest star on *Live with Mayor Apple*?"

"I didn't ask for any of this," Gail said. "But... I'm glad you're here."

Frank let the words hang there. Then he looked at her—really looked. There was sadness behind her eyes, but also something raw. Something real.

His eyes looked away.

"So..." he said, adjusting the collar, "how do I look?"

Gail studied him.

"Like they want you to," she said.

A pause settled between them, fragile and real.

"But your eyes—your eyes still look like you," Gail said quietly.

Outside, the motorcade engines rumbled to life, their growl echoing up the concrete walls, similar to a countdown. The city waited.

Their destination: Shake House—an interactive exhibit tucked inside the California Academy of Sciences, famous for simulating the full-body jolt of a major earthquake. But today, it wasn't tectonic plates that would shift. It was politics. Mayor Apple had chosen it as the symbolic birthplace of her newest crusade — the Apple Movement.

Frank looked down at the cue card in his hand. A single line, phonetically transcribed Spanish, stared back at him knowingly, as if it understood he didn't belong. The letters wobbled in his vision, smug little symbols daring him to trip. Around him, makeup brushes flicked, cue cards shuffled, and voices hummed with rehearsed urgency. But all Frank could feel was the weight of that one line—foreign, brittle, and ready to betray him on cue.

He looked up at Gail.

"Let's get this over with before someone asks me to salsa."

She grinned, the kind that barely lifted one corner of her mouth. "Too late. It's on the itinerary—right after the simulated 6.9 quake."

CHAPTER 22
AFTER SHOCKS

"If you can fake sincerity, you've got it made."

— GEORGE BURNS

The kiss of the rising sun lit up the dashboard of the first-generation Prius, ushering to life the majestic Golden Gate Bridge. Below the iconic span, the wind whipped the bay waters into a white-capped fury.

For Frank Wright, a deep, cleansing breath wasn't helping anymore. The air was thick, the lights were hot, and his role—whatever it was—kept slipping. People clapped. People stared. Something shifted. And when the cracks appeared, it wasn't truth that came rushing in. It was something else entirely.

The Shake House in San Francisco pulsed with carefully engineered energy. Once an immersive earthquake simulation designed to teach families about tectonic shifts, it had been repurposed for political theater. Today, it was ground zero for the launch of The Apple Movement—where staged tremors met the rumblings of a real political quake.

Campaign aides buzzed backstage, herding influencers, adjusting signage, and reviewing cue cards. The crowd beyond the curtain was growing restless, a sea of curated outfits and filtered expectations. Stage lights warmed the platform in slow, deliberate degrees.

On Frank, they were intentionally dimmed.

"Keep the lights soft on 'Javier,'" Mayor Apple said under her breath, turning slightly toward Pixel. "Let the vibe carry the moment. We're selling vision, not verification."

Pixel nodded without looking up, tapping a silent note onto her tablet.

Frank stood just behind the podium, posture straight but face tight, like someone posing for a photo at their own funeral. The tanner was holding—for now. But the AC in the Shake House was overworked, and beads of sweat were already forming along his hairline.

Gail stepped up beside him, polished and composed. She glanced at Frank and gave him a barely-there smile before turning to the crowd.

The spotlight found her—clean, centered, intentional. Stanford-approved.

"California has always been a land of movement. Of new ideas, bold risks, and shifting ground," she began, her voice carrying with calm conviction.

She paused, letting her silhouette hold the audience for a moment—backlit by the soft tremble of the simulation floor.

"Today, we shake things up for the right reasons. Not because we want to—but because we have to."

The floor vibrated gently beneath them, the designed tremor perfectly timed.

"We recognize that when the ground shifts beneath us, it doesn't signal collapse—it signals momentum. Progress. Renewal. And today, California stands not in fear of change but prepared to lead it."

Applause surged, cued by a discreet signal from Pixel in the wings. Frank smiled on command; eyes locked on some vague point in the distance.

Cameras burst with light.

He flinched.

A second drop of sweat rolled past his temple and took a bit of the spray tan with it, streaking faintly down his cheek. Ron, watching from the crowd, winced.

Frank leaned toward the mic—briefly.

"Gracias por estar aquí."

Just one line. Clean. Memorized. Enough to sell the image.

Pixel clapped first. The rest followed.

But behind the applause, one reporter in the third row leaned toward her colleague.

"Does he seem... off to you?"

His colleague shrugged.

Mayor Apple took the stage with theatrical command, her heels clicking across the Shake House platform like gavels. The spotlight locked on her, the room dimming just slightly around Frank—still smiling, still sweating, still trying to hold the illusion together as another droplet of spray tan slid from his forehead.

He could feel the light from above on him. Dim, yes. But not enough to hide everything.

"Thank you, Gail, for that powerful message," Mayor Apple began, voice strong and steady. "Today, we aren't here to fear the shaking—we're here to guide it. To make sure that when California moves, it moves with purpose, with unity, and with all its people."

Applause rose, dutiful but thinner this time.

Down in the press section, a sharp-eyed photographer from the *Golden Gate Ledger* lowered his camera, eyes narrowing as he stared at Frank as if running facial recognition software in his head.

"That's supposed to be 3E Javi, right?" he whispered.

"Yeah," his colleague replied, "the guy from Staton 11."

The reporter frowned. "That guy had a deeper voice and smiled like he knew secrets."

He paused.

"This guy looks as if he's in a hostage video."

Frank shifted uncomfortably. The heat lamps above made everything feel like a poorly ventilated interrogation room.

In the front row, a bored teen with oversized headphones suddenly blurted out, "Yo, that dude looks like Axe King from TikTok—but with a runnin' tan!"

Laughter rippled through a few rows. Frank felt it. All of it.

Ron, watching from stage right, straightened and made a slow, deliberate move toward the edge of the press area. His velvet jacket and "ASK ME ABOUT FIRE SAFETY" pin gave him the look of a well-meaning sideshow act—but his eyes were locked on the reporters like a chess player with his king in trouble.

Ron stepped forward casually, offering a bundle of folded shirts like they were diplomatic credentials.

"Hey there—media folks," he said, voice smooth. "I've got a few 3E T's Javi gave me to pass out. What sizes do you need?"

The *Golden Gate Ledger* reporter glanced at him and laughed.

"Back off, clown car."

On stage, Mayor Apple didn't flinch. She was in full rhythm now, her voice ringing with the conviction of someone who truly believed the performance was the product.

"We're not just rebuilding roads and bridges—we're rebuilding trust," she declared. "From firehouses to families. From fault lines to a California that doesn't crack."

A final wave of applause crested, louder this time—thanks to a subtle gesture from Pixel, who clapped as if she was trying to jolt a room full of mannequins to life.

Frank nodded, his smile locked in place even as his uniform collar clung to his skin and the truth lingered in the air, akin to a gas leak waiting for a spark.

The applause died down, but not the curiosity. The stage lights stayed dim over Frank—who was now visibly sweating, his tan patchy like a poorly frosted cake under heat lamps.

Pixel pressed a hand to her earpiece, muttering to comms.

"We skip Q&A. We skip Q&A..."

Mayor Apple smiled wide to the crowd.

"We've got time for a few quick questions before we break into our community engagement sessions."

The phrase “community engagement sessions” landed with the enthusiasm of a wet sock in a punch bowl. The press didn’t flinch. In fact, they leaned forward—microphones raised, eyes narrowing.

A reporter in the third row stood.

“Actually, this question’s for Javi.”

Mayor Apple’s smile froze. Pixel stopped mid-blink.

“You’ve appeared at a number of events,” the reporter continued, “but today… something’s different. Your voice, your posture—”

Frank blinked, suddenly aware of the lights, the cameras, and the three beads of sweat staging a jailbreak down his neck. He clutched his wrist, trying to steady it—right over left, a man playing the wrong part in his own body.

For a split second, the room became a stalled elevator.

Mayor Apple stepped in, smile tightening.

“He’s fine. A little warm—these lights are intense. But let’s not get distracted. We’re here to talk about shaking up California—with real solutions, not rumors.”

Frank nodded along, his smile strained, his brow now glistening like a wax statue under a heat lamp.

“He’s melting,” one reporter muttered.

The murmurs grew. Something wasn’t right, and everyone

could feel it. A hand shot up for another follow-up, when suddenly—

"I'm pregnant," Gail said, stepping forward into the mic.

A collective gasp rippled across the crowd. Journalists who had been foaming at the mouth seconds earlier now froze, pens hovering midair.

Frank stared at her—somewhere between baffled and betrayed. Gail gave him the kind of smile that said, *Don't worry, I'm saving your butt.*

The room held its breath. Even the DJ—poised to cue the post-speech playlist—froze with his finger over the play button.

And then—boom—Ron exploded onto the stage from stage right, a cannonball at a baptism. Arms flung wide, chest puffed, his grin burned with unearned confidence. He crashed into the spotlight as though he'd just bought a truckload of fireworks with someone else's credit card and couldn't wait to light the fuse indoors.

"Let's hear it for family, y'all!" he bellowed.

He began flinging freshly screen-printed *3E STRONG* T-shirts into the crowd like a proud uncle at a backyard quinceañera. One shirt smacked a city councilman in the face. Another landed squarely on a reporter's open laptop. Ron didn't notice—or care.

"Three E's!" he shouted, pointing both fingers skyward. *"Earthquakes, Equity, and Expecting!"*

For a few long seconds, the moment hung in the air like a balloon filled with questionable gas. Then—slowly, then suddenly—the crowd clapped. Someone even let out a cheer.

Mayor Apple gave Pixel a sideways glance of exhausted approval. Pixel, mid-cringe, simply nodded.

Frank wiped his brow, still stunned, and muttered under his breath, "I'm in hell. And they've got merch."

"You're welcome," Gail said, smiling.

Frank leaned in, voice low. "Wait, you're not able to…?"

Gail's expression didn't waver. She looked calm, composed, as if she'd just read off a weather report.

"We're excited. It's early, but—yes. Life moves fast. Sometimes, it shakes you up in ways you never expected."

A gentle wave of "awws" floated through the room, air freshener sprayed over a crime scene. The tension broke, if only slightly. The mood shifted.

Mayor Apple leaned toward Pixel, wide-eyed.

"Did you know?" she whispered.

"I do now," Pixel replied, equally hushed.

Gail kept smiling. Frank kept sweating. But the questions about Javi stopped—for now.

From the edge of the stage, Ron scooped up one of the tossed T-shirts and slung it over his shoulder, a prizefighter in a charity match. He turned to the press with a wide grin and said, "Just so we're clear—I'm officially representing the baby. Media inquiries, book deals, diaper endorsements… talk to me."

Pixel closed her eyes. Mayor Apple blinked twice. Frank sighed through his teeth.

And the music began.

CHAPTER 23

FAULT LINES

"The most common way people give up their power is by thinking they don't have any."

— **ALICE WALKER**, ANYTHING WE LOVE CAN BE SAVED

The kiss of the rising sun lit up the dashboard of the first-generation Prius, ushering to life the majestic Golden Gate Bridge. Below the iconic span, the wind whipped the bay waters into a white-capped fury.

For Frank Wright, a deep, cleansing breath felt more like taking inventory. What was still his? What had been borrowed? What had been taken? The ground had shaken—not just in San Francisco, but across California.

Some fractures show. Others stay hidden, waiting for the next shift.

Back at the loft, Frank sat hunched at the small kitchen table, peeling dried stage makeup from his neck like it was shedding guilt. His Shake House name tag—"JAVI" in bold all-caps—lay face-down next to a half-empty wine cooler.

Ron stood at the counter stirring instant noodles with the urgency of a surgeon and the outfit of a man who'd recently lost a bet—shirtless, in pajama pants, and still wearing his "3E STRONG" campaign lanyard.

Frank wiped his forehead, the paint streaked and running. "That wasn't a campaign stop. That was a four-alarm hostage drill."

Ron smirked, "Relax. You didn't save the city, you just sweated through some face paint. Very off-Broadway firefighter."

Frank shook his head. "I never should've agreed to this. It isn't me. I'm not a prop, not some rented backdrop for bad optics. I used to save lives—crawl into burning buildings, carry people out. Now I'm standing in borrowed shoes, pretending at something I don't even recognize. And while I sweat under stage lights, a mayor with more hunger than heart is twisting earthquake science into a campaign slogan—chasing votes from people too blind to see the ambition behind it all."

Ron slurped his noodles, unfazed. "Yeah, but you looked good doing it. That tan? Had real Rico Suave energy, my dude—as if you were about to drop a single and steal someone's girlfriend at a community pool."

Frank slowly shook his head, "I'm serious. Why am I even trying to get that job back? What's the point of going back to Station 11 if my helmet's just another political accessory? At any moment, someone like Javi can be inserted, and I'm deleted."

Ron interrupted, "Listen, amigo—it's because you want to serve. Do something real."

Frank exhaled, raising the wine cooler as if it were a white flag.

"Exactly. When did that stop being enough?"

Ron tossed his chopsticks onto the counter, finished with both dinner and diplomacy.

"Look, I get it," he said, his voice low. "You used to matter in ways that didn't need a spotlight. Now you're stuck under one—hoping the makeup holds, the accent lands, and nobody sees the cracks underneath. It's not just the lies wearing you down. It's that quiet question in the back of your head: What if this version of me is the only one they'll accept?"

Frank sat down on the couch, eyes heavy.

"I don't know what I'm doing anymore, man. Feels like I'm just background noise in my own life. Everything's upside down—I've got no money, and my dates are either football crazies, tarot junkies, or Greek island hoppers. Even Shiela-slash-Aleihs looks normal right now."

Ron moved toward Frank, his tone dropping from flippant to unexpectedly sincere.

"Hey—let's go back to Tammy Lynn," Ron said.

Frank didn't even lift his head. "Ughh..."

"Right, anyway—bowling pin tattoo, a laugh that could deflate a bouncy house..."

Frank gave him a side glance.

"Then the call comes. Nothing dramatic. Just: it's over. Oh, and you can keep Grandma's jalapeños."

Frank winced. "Yeah, I remember."

"Turns out she'd met Dale the Trucker down at Split Happens. Chrome stacks on his rig, red-white-and-blue bowling ball, Spotify fifty-fifty between outlaw country and libertarian rants. And of course—he's married to Joline."

Frank nodded, a man stuck in a Twilight Zone rerun. "Got it...again. She took Joline's man. Celebrity pyramid stuff."

But Ron's voice shifted, the humor draining out. "The point is—I gave away my power. That's what I didn't see until it was too late. I was so focused on how she made me feel—validated, seen, less broken—that I forgot what she saw in me to begin with."

He tapped his chest once, sharp and certain, as if he'd finally located the source of the loss.

"It wasn't my bowling form or my dumb one-liners. It was my energy, Frank. My presence. I walked into a room and people lit up. That's mojo. And once it's gone... you're rudderless. Just drifting."

Frank tilted his head. "Mojo, huh?"

He let the silence hang for a moment before continuing.

"It's what you're doing with Mayor Apple. You think she's offering you a shot at redemption. But she's not. She needs you. You've got the story, the face, the credibility she can't buy."

"Reclaim your mojo, amigo," he said, not waiting for permission. "You think this whole thing with Mayor Apple is some kind of cosmic second chance—but it's not. She doesn't want *you*. She wants your image. Your story. Your credibility to her campaign. She needs you to sell the narrative that gets her to Sacramento."

Frank stared at the floor, but Ron wasn't done.

"And Gail? She needs you too—just not the real you. She needs the man she married. The stable, loyal, backbone-of-the-community version of you. The guy in the uniform, not the guy in this loft peeling off stage makeup and sipping wine-flavored shame."

Frank looked up sharply, the words landing harder than he expected.

"You think they're offering you something," Ron continued. "But they're not. They're cashing in. And you—somewhere along the way—you stopped asking what *you* need. You just started playing the roles."

Frank's voice was low. "So, what, I'm supposed to just walk away?"

"No," Ron said, arms folded. "I'm saying wake up! You keep wondering why none of this feels right? It's 'cause you're living other people's versions of you. Mayor Apple's puppet. Gail's husband's hologram. You gave them the keys, man. I'm just saying—maybe it's time you take the keys back."

The loft went quiet except for the hum of the old fridge and the soft fizz of Frank's wine cooler. He didn't say anything, but his fingers tightened around the bottle, like he'd just remembered it was in his hand.

Outside, the neon sign from the vape shop stuttered in the night—less a light than a question, wavering between fading out and burning through.

Somewhere across town, aspiration buzzed at a higher frequency.

The mayor's office was bright and orderly, though the hour made the fluorescent lights feel harsher than usual. Papers were stacked in careful piles—cue cards, voter data printouts, schedules waiting to be memorized. Half-finished green juices sat on coasters, the condensation leaving faint rings on the wood.

Mayor Apple paced in her red-soled heels, steady and deliberate, as if each step were part of the campaign itself.

Gail sat at the table, composed but clearly running on adrenaline. Pixel stood near the digital campaign board, arms crossed, eyes darting between tabs labeled "Post-Shake Damage Control" and "Backup Javier Protocol."

"I mean—wow," Mayor Apple said, gesturing with a tablet. "That was a full-blown seismic event. Campaign-shaking. And you, Gail... you stuck the landing like a gymnast with a law degree."

She paused, smile widening.

"I could see you in Sacramento with me. 3E division. Or better. Once we seal this thing in two weeks."

"I'm just glad I could help," Gail replied, smiling carefully. "Crisis improvisation wasn't on the job description."

"Well, we got lucky," Pixel added. "Frank was sweating like a tourist in Death Valley, and one more follow-up question would've turned that podium into a confession booth. He's gonna crack, I can feel it."

Mayor Apple nodded. "He's not built for this. He's a fireman, not a shapeshifter. But we needed the look, and he gave us that—for now."

"He's stronger than you think," Gail said, voice steady. "I've seen him pull people out of fires—real ones. When everything's falling apart, Frank doesn't fold. He focuses."

Pixel looked unconvinced, but the mayor studied Gail for a beat.

"Fine. I'll take your word for it... for now. But, Pixel—"

She turned, her tone sharpening.

"I want a contingency plan. A clean, press-ready, 'nothing to see here' pivot. We've got the lead. The finish line's in sight. Let's not blow it because Firefighter Frank forgets which accent he's using."

Pixel nodded, already on her phone.

"Also—contact Jax. My little guy from Station 11. He's got charisma. People love him. He's a human step stool—small, sturdy, and surprisingly useful."

"For the 3E slogan?" Pixel asked.

"Exactly. Earthquakes, Equity, and... Everyone Counts. Even the pocket-sized ones."

Pixel tried not to laugh but failed. Gail just raised an eyebrow.

"You saved the day with a fake baby announcement," Mayor Apple added. "It was fake, right?"

"Heaven, yes."

Gail's answer hung in the air like a final pin dropping. The mayor, mid-scroll through polling charts, paused and looked back over her shoulder.

"Shame," Apple said, smirking. "Could've been a nice bump for us—no pun intended."

Apple didn't wait for a reply—she never did. With a flick of her wrist, the tablet closed, and the moment was over.

As the mayor's town car eased into traffic and rolled toward the Bay Bridge, Gail sat alone in the backseat, hands folded neatly in her lap. City lights flickered across the windshield—brief glimmers of a world still moving. The only sound was the soft hum of the engine and the quiet churn of her own thoughts.

She should've felt triumphant. The mayor had just floated a future in Sacramento—3E Division, maybe more. Eight months ago, she would've laughed at the idea. But now? It didn't feel so far-fetched.

Outside the tinted windows, San Francisco drifted past—Mission, Valencia, Van Ness—streets threaded with memories she and Frank had built. Some joyful. Some heavy. All real.

Her phone buzzed on the seat beside her. She let it go.

She had left Stanford for him, surrendering the chance to become the woman she'd come west to be, trading it for the safety of someone else's world. She had loved him—maybe still did—but the cost had been her own life. Now the mayor was offering something different. Maybe even what she had been searching for when she first set foot in California. A way forward that finally felt like her own.

She adjusted her posture, suddenly aware of how different she looked now. The heels. The tailored blazer. Her voice now quoted in political blogs. This wasn't the life she imagined—but it was the one she'd built, piece by piece, in the absence of the one that fell apart.

This isn't Kansas, she thought. *And I'm not the girl who left campus with a suitcase full of promises.*

The car turned toward her neighborhood. The silence grew louder.

Frank had changed. So had she.

The only question now was—had they changed too far in opposite directions?

As the car slowed to a stop, she took a breath, smoothed her jacket, and stepped out into the cool night air. Not just a wife. Not just a fixer. And certainly not just a woman with a fake baby bump.

But someone who might finally be stepping into her own story.

CHAPTER 24
THREE'S A FARE

"Life can only be understood backwards; but it must be lived forwards."

— SØREN KIERKEGAARD

The kiss of the rising sun lit up the dashboard of the first-generation Prius, ushering to life the majestic Golden Gate Bridge. Below the iconic span, the wind whipped the bay waters into a white-capped fury.

For Frank Wright, a deep, cleansing breath didn't steady him so much as slow the spin. Some rides were quiet. Some came with baggage. Sometimes, his drives felt like emotional bumper cars—no brakes, no map, and no one admitting where they were really headed.

The hum of the Prius blended with the low thump of the road beneath him. Frank's hands rested on the wheel, knuckles pale, eyes flicking between the street ahead and the dull glow of the rideshare app. The car smelled faintly of breath mints and tanner. He'd flipped his "fun driver facts" card around—no one needed to know he'd once run into a three-alarm blaze just to save a stack of untouched takeout menus.

The soft shimmer of the city framed his thoughts like bookends. Ron's words lingered, chewing at him since the loft.

You've got the power, amigo. Not her. She needs you to be the good soldier. But what if the soldier's not on her side anymore?

Frank cracked the window. Cool night air slipped in, brushing his cheek. The kind of air that made you believe things could change—even if you still smelled like drugstore bronzer and faint regret.

He idled in the pickup lane, the radio low, a gas station ice coffee sweating beside him in the cupholder. He scrolled through old texts with his thumb, pausing on one from weeks ago:

Safe travels! I'll be there when you land. –F

A new message popped up.

Nancy: "Landed! Just got my bags :) Can't wait to see you!"

Frank swallowed hard. That message had been sent by a previous version of himself—pre-tanner, pre-NDA, pre-Javi. Before campaign rallies, fake accents, and wardrobe fittings. Back when pretending wasn't part of his daily routine.

He spotted her through the windshield. Nancy, fresh off the terminal escalator, wrapped in breezy linen and a post-Greek glow. She looked like the cover of a novel titled *Heartbreak Hotel—Elvis Edition*. Golden tan, white hat tucked under her arm, and a relaxed wave as she made her way toward the car. Frank rolled down the window. "Hey—sorry, the front's a disaster. Mind hopping in the back?"

Nancy slid into the backseat with her bags and an easy smile.

"Frank! Look at you. You're glowing..." She paused, squinting slightly. "Wait—are you bronzed?"

"Sunlight and shame," Frank said, easing the car from the curb. "Welcome home."

She laughed, settling in. "It's good to be back. Greece was wild. My friend Eleni met a goat farmer-slash-DJ. We'll see how that plays out."

Frank smiled, eyes on the road. "You were gone a while."

"Yeah, well... two weeks turns into forever when you lose your passport and find bottomless ouzo."

Her phone buzzed. She picked it up, already mid-scroll as

she launched into another story. Frank's rideshare app pinged at the same time.

DING—New Ride Request.

Pickup: Mission District. 7 minutes away.

He glanced at the screen, then back at Nancy.

"Mind if I take this one? Quick detour. Shouldn't be out of the way."

"Sure, go for it," she said, waving him off as she continued her call.

Frank tapped *Accept* without checking the name and turned east, deeper into the swirl of San Francisco.

Whatever this ride was, it felt similar to a brief detour from the double life he'd been pretending wasn't unraveling. Or maybe—just maybe—it was a reminder that something real still existed beneath the makeup and politics.

Only when he pulled up outside *Salsa Live* did he glance down at the name on the screen.

Stefania T.

"You've gotta be kidding me," Frank muttered.

Before he could process it, the studio door swung open.

There she was.

Same electric smile. Same kinetic spark.

Stefania strode toward the Prius in salsa heels, cheeks flushed from the rhythm still coursing through her. She slid into the backseat without looking up.

“Hey—just a quick ride to Valencia and 18th. Late dinner thing,” she said, catching her breath.

Frank’s eyes found hers in the rearview mirror.

“Uh… you sure? Looks like you’re heading away from the party?”

She looked up, paused... and blinked.

“Frank?”

She leaned forward, her eyes wide.

“Hey, Stefania,” he said quietly.

“Are you serious?” she asked, voice flat with disbelief.

Frank half-smiled, hands gripping the wheel at ten and two, every muscle tense.

“Yeah… life’s got a weird sense of humor lately.”

"Wow," Stefania said, her voice soft with surprise. "You know, just last night I thought about you. I was looking at the stars through my telescope—don’t laugh, it’s therapeutic—and I actually wondered… is fate real?"

She paused.

"I didn’t expect this answer."

In the backseat, Nancy chuckled into her phone, still mid-conversation.

"Yeah, totally. Just landed. I'll send pics when I get home."

She ended the call and turned to Stefania beside her, eyes bright with curiosity.

"Oh! Hi, do you two know each other?"

Stefania nodded casually. "Yes, we met online. We've been ghosting each other since going out a couple of times."

Nancy tilted her head, smiling playfully but with a hint of edge. "Interesting. I mean, I've only known him a short while, but I wouldn't peg him as a ghoster."

"Oh, he's got range," Stefania replied, matching her tone. "Firefighter, part-time philosopher, now full-time man of mystery with a side hustle in awkward reunions."

Nancy laughed. "Sounds like I missed the whole first act."

"We went axe-throwing on our first date," Stefania added. "Nothing says romance like drinks and sharp objects."

"Charming. I'm Nancy, by the way. Just got back from Greece. Met Frank at a fire safety class."

"Ok, yea, right," Stefania said with a small, deliberate smile. "I'm Stefania."

The temperature in the car shifted. The banter thinned into silence.

Frank exhaled as the Prius crept uphill, two women in the backseat, and no exit strategy in sight.

Frank's hands rested on the steering wheel a little tighter than necessary, as if it were the only steady thing he could count on. The Prius slid quietly through the Mission, its cabin a reluctant confessional. Headlights brushed across puddles of neon and broken dreams, the streets reflecting more than he cared to admit.

In the back seat sat Nancy on one side, Stefania on the other —an unlikely carpool engineered by fate, sly enough to feel like coincidence but certain enough to feel planned.

Across the bridge in Sausalito, the full moon cast a quiet shimmer over the bay as the mayor's town car pulled into Gail's driveway.

She slid the key into the lock and eased open the tall double doors, their oak panels and iron handles too stately for how small she felt just now. They gave way with a muted creak, and she stepped inside, shoulders slumping beneath the aftershock of the Shake House. Outwardly, she'd saved the day—pregnant, radiant, the campaign's sudden heroine. Inwardly, she carried nothing but the lie. All she wanted now was silence.

She kicked off her heels and moved toward the kitchen—only to stop short.

Javi stood barefoot at the counter, humming off-key and peeling a mango with monastic focus. On the small TV tucked in the corner, a muted broadcast of the Shake House, along with footage from the Dodgers game—his ceremonial first pitch. Clean delivery. Smooth roll into the catcher's mitt.

Gail blinked.

"¿Dónde has estado, Javi?" she asked, voice sharp with disbelief.

He looked up and grinned, mango juice glistening down his thumb.

"Estaba con la chica... del maquillaje," he said. "You know? Pretty eyes. Lashes like... ventiladores. She say, 'Come.' So I come. We go, music, kissing, poquito dancing. Then... puff. She gone."

"Gone?" Gail stepped forward, incredulous. "Javi, you disappeared! For two weeks! We thought you'd been—"

Javi patted his heart with exaggerated sincerity. "No muerto. Just... romántico."

He gestured to the TV with a piece of mango peel, still smiling.

"Pero él—Frank. I see. He is me! Bueno, no tan guapo... pero close. Muy close."

"You saw the broadcast?" Gail asked, her voice caught somewhere between confusion and dread.

"Sí, sí. Cantina. Muy impresionante," Javi said, still grinning. "He walk like me. Talk... casi like me. Frank muy brave, like bombero. But with... más gel in hair."

He held out a slice of mango, sticky and golden. "Want? Sweet."

Gail slowly sat at the kitchen table, staring at him like a riddle she'd forgotten how to solve.

"Ay, Javier…" she sighed. "You've made un gran lío. A big mess."

Javi stood there like he'd never left, comfortably humming as he slid the knife cleanly through the mango's flesh.

"Maybe... dosis Javier's, eh?" he added, not looking up.

Gail blinked, stunned. Then she reached for her phone.

TEXT FROM GAIL (Group Chat):

> Javi's back. And in my kitchen!!

She hit send with shaky fingers just as Javi, completely unbothered, peeled another mango like it was a normal Tuesday.

TEXT FROM PIXEL (appeared instantly):

> WHAT?!

> Keep him there. I'm serious, Gail—don't let him leave. Not even to pee.

Tell him you have mucho salsa. Tie his shoelaces together. I don't care—just STALL.

Gail looked up.

Javi winked. Juice dripped from his fingers.

"California buried him," she muttered. "Now he's back like a zombie with PR training."

Within minutes, there was a knock—three sharp raps, no hesitation.

Before she could stand, the front door opened with polished urgency. Pixel swept in, flanked by a trio in matching gray polos stamped *CITY TASK FORCE*. One of them with a Bluetooth earpiece was speaking into the cuff of his jacket, murmuring code words. Another approached Javi and gently removed the half-eaten mango from his hand as if it were contraband.

Gail blinked. "What the—?"

"Don't worry," Pixel said, her eyes drifting across the room the way an algorithm combs a data set, pulling out what mattered. "We're here for him."

Javi straightened instinctively, dabbing mango juice from his chin with the back of his hand. "¿Todo bien?"

Pixel didn't answer. Her gaze stayed locked on her tablet as she called to her team, "Get the car ready." Then to Gail:

"We'll debrief tomorrow. Mayor's office. Nine a.m. sharp. Don't be late."

One of the agents handed Javi a city-branded windbreaker as they began herding him toward the door—firm, but with the practiced gentleness of a team that specialized in quiet removals.

At the threshold, silhouetted in the porch light, Javi paused and turned, his voice ringing with pride and something unexpectedly tender.

"He estado practicando mi brazo para lanzar más pelotas de béisbol para la campaña," he said.

Gail watched as they whisked him into the night like a scandal with legs.

Then silence.

The kitchen smelled of mango and confusion. She looked down at the counter.

They'd even taken the knife.

Back across town, Frank kept his eyes on the road but, somehow, felt the urge to swipe.

Despite the quiet meltdown unfolding in his Prius, Ron's words echoed in his head—*"Don't let them take your power, amigo."*

Maybe it was pathetic, maybe it was survival, but swiping felt like the last thing he had any power over. It wasn't about connection anymore. It was distance. Distraction. A thumb-sized illusion of choice.

Nancy sat in the backseat, scrolling through sun-drenched photos of Santorini, sighing after each one. Stefania, arms crossed, stared moodily out the opposite window.

"So... uh," Frank started, voice creaking like an old screen door, "I just want to say I'm kind of... new at this. The whole dating thing."

Neither woman moved.

"I've been out of the game for almost twenty years," he continued. "Just trying to keep my head above water since my wife kicked me out."

That did it.

Nancy snapped her head up, eyes wide. "Excuse me?"

Stefania turned, slower—like an actress in a horror film. "Still married?"

Frank glanced into the rearview mirror, trying to beat the yellow light without looking like he was trying to beat the yellow light. His voice dropped, low and guilty, as if he were confessing directly to the steering wheel.

"Well, technically—yeah, legally—I'm still married."

He lifted both hands briefly from the wheel, palms up, like a man demonstrating a magic trick gone wrong. "Separated!

Emotionally. Physically. Spiritually. I sleep on an inflatable mattress in a room with no closet."

Nancy's voice sliced through the air from the back seat. "So, this was your rebound tour?"

"No! More like... online discovery," Frank replied, eyes locked on the road, pride clearly left behind somewhere at airport arrivals. "Look, my wife dumped me for the same guy who stole my job at the fire station. That freakin' Javier, he's made my life—"

Nancy cut in, her tone suddenly piqued. "You mean Javi? The dreamy migrant firefighter in Mayor Apple's commercials?"

Frank winced. "Yeah. Him."

There was a beat of silence before Stefania spoke, her voice tight and glacial. "Why didn't you mention you were separated on **Love.com**?"

Frank exhaled sharply. "It's complicated. My buddy told me not to get too heavy in the profile. He also said chicks dig shirtless pics and holding dead fish, so... yeah. I might've misread the whole online dating thing."

The Prius slowed to a stop in front of La Reina Roja, a lively cantina spilling warm light and laughter onto the sidewalk. String lights dangled overhead, and the faint echo of mariachi drifted from inside.

"This is me," Stefania said, unbuckling without looking at him.

Nancy reached for her door handle, paused, and gave Frank a once-over. "You know what? Suddenly, I'm in the mood for a margarita. I'll make it from here."

With bags in tow, she stepped out, linking arms with Stefania as the two disappeared into the glow of the cantina —heels tapping with a rhythm that seemed to sweep away the entire ride, the conversation, and any chance Frank had hoped to keep.

He sat in silence, blinking at the empty backseat.

"I just got dumped by two women at the same time," he muttered. "Is that... progress?"

His phone buzzed.

Ride completed.

Tip: Optional.

Rating: ★☆☆☆☆ – Loser. – Stefania

Frank stared at the screen like it had slapped him.

He sighed, slipped the Prius into drive, and pulled into the night—heart heavy, wallet light, and now officially one star closer to rock bottom.

As he rolled up to the next red light, his phone buzzed again in the console.

RON CALLING.

Frank hesitated, then hit the speaker.

"Dude," Ron's voice burst through the car, practically vibrating with excitement. "You ready? I just trademarked the name—Cyrano."

Frank blinked. "What is that?"

"Our new app," Ron said, dead serious. "AI-powered date whisperer. It listens in on your date and talks you through it in real time. Like an earpiece life coach... but with attitude."

Frank stared blankly at the road ahead. "You want to put a robot in my ear while I'm on a date?"

"Yes! It detects awkward silences, yellow flags, red flags, and suggests emotionally intelligent responses—or excuses to leave. It even adjusts tone. You want charming? It's charming. You want mysterious? Boom—Cyrano switches to jazz mode."

Frank exhaled. "You named it *Cyrano*? Like... *de Bergerac*?"

"It's a mashup of romance, daring, and... I don't know, something with panache. Focus groups will love it."

Frank made a right turn onto a quiet street, shaking his head. "Ron, you're a TED Talk that ran headfirst into a Craigslist ad!"

There was a pause on the line.

"So?"

Frank's voice dropped. "Well, I could've used it ten minutes ago—right before Stefania and Nancy dumped me at the same time."

A beat.

"*What?!*" Ron exploded.

"I'll tell you when I get back," Frank said, staring into the bay night.

The light turned green. He drove on, wondering if Cyrano could talk him through the wreckage of his life.

CHAPTER 25
SURVEYS AND CONFESSIONALS

"Stay gold, Ponyboy. Stay gold..."

—**JOHNNY CADE**, THE OUTSIDERS BY S.E. HINTON

The kiss of the rising sun lit up the dashboard of the first-generation Prius, ushering to life the majestic Golden Gate Bridge. Below the iconic span, the wind whipped the bay waters into a white-capped fury.

For Frank Wright, a deep, cleansing breath used to feel noble. Now it felt... naive. Truth had become a kind of currency—overspend it, and you end up broke.

Some people lied to get ahead. Others just trimmed the truth until it looked more photogenic.

City Hall buzzed with low-level urgency—the kind that hummed beneath marble floors. Gail followed Pixel down a corridor lined with campaign posters and fresh flower arrangements meant to disguise panic.

Inside the executive conference room, Mayor Apple stood at the head of the table, arms crossed, caffeine pulsing in her veins. She didn't greet Gail. She just gestured to the seat across from her.

"Close the door," Apple said to Pixel. "Let's move fast."

Gail sat, already sensing the shift in the air—cool, decisive, corporate. A woman ready to put a bow on a crisis.

"We've made a decision," the mayor said, her tone crisp and final. "After internal review, image testing, and about three sleepless nights... we're going with Javi."

Gail blinked. "To do what, exactly?"

"Be seen," Apple replied. "That's it. I've got the biggest debate of my political career in two days, and I need visual certainty—no surprises, no liabilities. Javi stands next to me during the post-debate photo op. Maybe a wave. No talking. And heaven help him if he flirts."

Pixel gave a small, strained smile. "We've prepped him on stillness."

Apple nodded. "He doesn't need to speak. He just needs to remind voters what progress looks like."

Pixel nodded, flipping through slides on her tablet. "We're calling it *Silent Strength.* His image polls off the charts. Latino voters see themselves in him. Suburban women think he's emotionally available. Independents think he looks like he recycles."

Mayor Apple leaned forward, fingers steepled. "It's not about what he says—it's the face. The commercials made him familiar. Familiar equals trustworthy. That's all most voters need."

Gail let out a slow breath. "So where does that leave Frank?"

Apple offered a tight smile. "Nowhere."

Gail sat up straighter. "Wait—what?"

"We're cutting him loose," Apple said, like she was canceling lunch. "He served his purpose. He made a comeback, got us through for five minutes, and now we pivot. He doesn't belong in this final stretch."

Gail stiffened. "But you told him—"

"I told him we'd revisit his position after the campaign," Apple interrupted. "And we have. Frank's a relic. A straight, middle-aged man with a hard hat—he screams backwards. That's not the image we're selling."

"To whom?" Gail asked, her voice low and flat.

Apple's smile returned, thinner now. "To everyone ready to embrace the future."

Pixel glanced up from her screen but said nothing.

"He doesn't belong in the SFFD anymore," Apple went on. "Not with the direction we're taking. We need a government and its apparatus that reflects the future—diverse, dynamic, forward-facing. Not someone who thinks it's still 1999."

Gail blinked. "So 'diverse'—as long as it's photogenic, easy to manage, and doesn't challenge your talking points."

Apple tilted her head. "Don't twist this. We're building equity."

"You're building optics," Gail shot back. "And Frank doesn't fit the packaging for California."

Apple studied her for a moment. The polished veneer cracked—just slightly—revealing something colder beneath. Something calculating. And maybe, faintly, impressed.

"California is evolving," she said, coolly. "For the greater good."

Gail leaned back, silent now, letting it all settle. The moment didn't need repeating—it had already carved itself into the room.

Not evolution—erasure.

Apple watched Gail for a beat longer, then gave a slight smile—almost a private acknowledgment.

"As I told you," she said, her tone quieter, "I need more people like you around me. Ones who don't just nod like

Pixel. We're this close to Sacramento. Just do your part and stop worrying about Frank. He's resilient."

Pixel looked up from her phone, smiled, then slipped wordlessly back into her digital cocoon.

Gail didn't respond right away. Her gaze lingered on the polished conference table, where her reflection stared back —warped and rippling across the glossy surface like the truth they were all trying to contain.

Outside, a breeze stirred along the Embarcadero, rustling the palm trees that lined the boulevard—tall, symmetrical, and not native to the city. They'd been planted for optics, like everything else lately. Imported beauty. Manufactured calm.

In Oakland, another kind of stillness was settling in.

Frank slouched on Ron's thrift-store sectional like a man recently ejected from a moving vehicle. One sock on, one foot bare. A half-drunk can of carbonated water sweated on the chipped coffee table as if it, too, carried regrets.

"Let me get this straight," Ron said, pacing near the incense shelf with the air of a disappointed guidance counselor before dropping into the seat beside Frank. "You told both of them… you're still married?"

Frank exhaled. "Yeah. I was trying to be honest. I told them

Gail and I aren't technically divorced. That it's… complicated."

Ron's face twisted, as if he'd just licked a nine-volt battery. "What did they say?"

"Nancy asked if this was my rebound tour. Stefania just went silent."

Ron shook his head. "Amigo, this is modern dating—not a confessional. You don't confess. You curate."

Frank blinked. "What does that mean?"

"It means you handed them a loaded weapon." Ron gestured as if he were a magician unveiling a bad trick. "Never full disclosure. Always intrigue. There's a reason guys shave five years off their age and call themselves retired spelunkers or semi-pro harpists. Even former Big & Tall models. You know what they're not? Completely honest."

He gasped, mock-horrified. "Honesty is a cry for help."

Ron grabbed his phone and started scrolling. "Don't believe me? Here—**LoveEmAndLeaveEm.com** says 84% of women claim to want honesty. That's the polls talking. Meanwhile, the profiles tell another story: they're swiping on guys named Jimmy who refer to themselves in the third person. What actually trends? Height. Job title. Adventurous keywords."

He looked up, deadpan. "Nobody clicks on 'Still Legally Married.'"

Frank scratched his head. "Wait—how are they measuring this? Women just answering polls between Pilates and podcasts?"

Ron leaned back, arms behind his head. "You're assuming women tell the truth. That's your first mistake. Polls are like horoscopes—vague, flattering, and designed to sell wine subscriptions. Profiles? That's performance art. The same woman who says she wants honesty has Botox and filler keeping her face together. Profile pics with three filters, and she'll swear she values the real you. That's claiming fluency in French because you once ordered fries in Montreal."

Frank leaned back. "So, I should've lied."

"No," Ron said, "You should've told a *better* truth. 'I was married. I learned from it. I'm ready now.' Instead, you handed them a press release titled: *Frank Wright—Now with 30% more self-awareness!*"

Frank looked over, sheepish. "Seriously?"

Ron nodded with the weariness of an elementary school teacher. "Modern women don't want a fixer-upper. They want a fully renovated emotional adult with Wi-Fi and hardwoods. You, my friend, showed up like a listing that says, 'plumbing uncertain, but has potential.'"

Frank squinted. "So, I should lean into 'potential.'"

Ron shrugged. "Potential gets you one sympathy swipe and a podcast mention. Maybe."

He crossed his arms. "You reveal an open wound and expect applause. You really think women are scrolling past startup founders, dog dads, and exotic mixologists just to land on a guy who says, 'Still legally married, but spiritually exhausted and open to vibes'?"

Frank rubbed his eyes. "So… women are being dishonest too?"

Ron shook his head. "Not dishonest. Strategic. We're all just out here cosmetic shopping—one illusion away from a meltdown."

Frank stared at the ceiling, eyes clouded. "So, what's the point? If you can't even be honest about who you are without it boomeranging back with judgment strapped to it like a grenade."

Ron smirked. "There is no point. It's not about truth—it's about traction. Dating is branding. And right now, you're coming off like a discontinued product."

Frank's phone buzzed on the armrest. He picked it up, read the screen aloud:

> "Hey Frank—just a heads-up. We're good on the Javi front. No longer need the stand-in. Mayor Apple really appreciated your cooperation. She'll be in touch. —Pixel."

He stared at the message, thumb hovering in midair.

Ron leaned over, peeking. "What does—'we're good' mean? Like, *good-good*? Or *politely-screw-off* good?"

Frank didn't answer right away. He just kept staring at the message, thumb idle.

"I don't know," he muttered. "She said, 'Appreciated your cooperation' like I donated a kidney. And 'she'll be in touch'... sounds like the last thing someone says before vanishing forever."

Ron sat up straighter. "Okay—but are you getting your job back or not?"

Frank shrugged. "No clue. It's like they ended a conversation I wasn't even part of."

Ron pointed at the phone. "Text back. Ask directly."

"I'm not begging the mayor's assistant for clarity like I'm waiting on a second date."

Ron held up a hand, deadpan. "More importantly—do we still get the 49ers tickets?"

Frank looked at him.

CHAPTER 26
THE DEBATE

"All I wanted was a Pepsi, just one Pepsi, and she wouldn't give it to me!"

— **SUICIDAL TENDENCIES,**
"INSTITUTIONALIZED" (1983)

The kiss of the rising sun lit up the dashboard of the first-generation Prius, ushering to life the majestic Golden Gate Bridge. Below the iconic span, the wind whipped the bay waters into a white-capped fury.

For Frank Wright, a deep, cleansing breath had once meant control. Now it ticked like a time bomb—each inhale just another wire waiting to be tripped.

Sacramento's downtown arena buzzed with lights, lanyards, and last-minute hairspray.

One week from Election Day, and California's political theater had rolled out the red carpet for its headliners.

Inside, media teams scurried, a swarm of caffeinated ants. Protesters outside shouted in six competing hashtags. And on every regional news channel, a digital countdown ticked toward the final gubernatorial debate:

> **Mayor Apple vs. Dean "The Glove" Banjo**—a San Diego baseball legend turned fiscal crusader with dimples, discipline, and a statewide fan base.

Backstage, two figures slipped past the first layer of security with alarming ease.

Frank walked briskly in his firefighter formal uniform—a pressed jacket, polished buttons, the look of ceremony rather than service. It wasn't his anymore, just borrowed back for optics, zipped tight to the collar. Beside him, Ron wore a crisp polo under a navy blazer embroidered with a knockoff "`Metro Crisis Unit`" logo and a laminated *Crisis Consultant Ron* badge that looked one paper jam away from disintegration.

At a second checkpoint, security barely lifted their eyes. One guard glanced up, caught the shine of Frank's jacket, and nodded without hesitation.

"Javi. You're good."

And that was it—no questions, no checks, just the kind of blind confidence that passes for vigilance.

They were waved through, oblivious to the fact that the real Javi was already in the dressing room with the mayor.

"Total chaos," Ron muttered. "Badge is doing all the work."

Frank adjusted his collar. "They see what they need. We're just playing along."

Without breaking stride, he and Ron pushed through the dressing room door marked:

APPLE / CAMPAIGN TEAM ONLY

Pixel nearly dropped her tablet. "Frank?! What are you—how—?!"

Mayor Apple spun from the mirror, lip gloss wand frozen mid-air. "You've got to be kidding me."

Inside, Gail sat silently in the corner, arms folded. Javier stood proudly at center stage of the chaos, grinning ear to ear and holding a glossy 8x10.

"¡Frank! ¡Hermano!" he cried, rushing over. "Bueno—we same! *La misma energía,* hombre."

He shoved the photo into Frank's hands. It was Dean "The Glove" Banjo, smiling in a tailored blazer, mid-handshake.

Across the front, scrawled in thick black Sharpie:

To Javier, mi amigo. Respect.
—Dean "The Glove" Banjo

Ron blinked. "You got a signed picture from the guy running against your boss?"

Javier beamed. "He say I have calves like a pitcher."

Frank didn't smile. He turned to Apple.

"Mayor. I need to know. Right now. Am I getting my job back or not?"

Her expression stiffened instantly. "You really want to have this conversation in a green room—ten minutes before I go live on statewide television?"

"You used me when it helped your campaign," Frank said, voice steady. "When it was convenient. Now the optics have shifted, and I've been erased. I deserve better."

Pixel winced. "Frank, now's not the time—"

"It's exactly the time," Ron cut in, stepping forward, arms folded across his borrowed blazer. "What better moment to talk about accountability than before the cameras start rolling?"

Apple glanced around the room. Gail held her gaze. Javier clutched his signed photo like it was scripture. Pixel's eyes darted nervously to the stage manager now hovering nearby, headset askew, tension rising.

Gail spoke at last, calm and clear. "You owe him the truth, Mayor. He didn't ask to be dragged into this. You made him a prop."

Apple let out a slow breath through her nose. "Fine. After the debate. We'll talk. In my office. No press. No staff."

Frank shook his head, adding a stern gaze while reaching into his pocket.

"No. We talk now."

Frank pulled a folded sheet of paper from his pocket, walked over, and set it gently on the makeup table in front of the mayor.

"Standard reinstatement," he said. "Position, salary, pension continuity. All it needs is your signature."

Apple stared at the document like it was radioactive.

"I'm not bluffing," Frank added. "If you don't sign it, I walk out there and give the press a real story—about a firefighter who got replaced, rebranded, and recycled in the name of the Apple Movement."

Ron gave a low whistle from across the room. "I knew I should've brought popcorn."

Apple's eyes narrowed. "You're blackmailing me?"

"No," Frank said evenly. "I'm forcing a moment of integrity."

The room froze. Even the stage manager stood motionless in the doorway, headset in hand.

Finally, Apple snatched a pen from the counter, clicked it hard, and signed with a defiant flourish. She paused for a moment, then scribbled something in the margin. Holding the document up between two fingers, she met Frank's eyes.

"You'll get your job back. But not in San Francisco."

Frank frowned. "Where, then?"

"Orange County," she said coolly. "Where you're from. Consider it a fresh start. Lower profile. Less press."

Frank studied her a moment longer. "So I get to serve again. But far enough away not to mess with your image."

Apple turned for one last look in the mirror. "And take off that uniform before you leave. We can't have you and Javi spotted in the same hallway."

He took the paper, folded it once, and slid it into his back pocket. "Alright."

From the door, the stage manager raised his voice. "One minute!"

Pixel scrambled to grab Apple's debate binder and thrust it into her hands.

Ron leaned over to Frank as they headed out of the room and toward the exit. "Orange County? Back to your roots, right?"

From inside, Javi shot his fist into the air — part defiance, part drama — a one-man Breakfast Club in Spanish. "¡Vamos, hermano! ¡Bravo!"

As showtime approached, the lights inside the arena dimmed to a patriotic hue.

Spotlights flared. Intro music swelled.

Two podiums. Two candidates. One week from decision day.

At stage left: Mayor Apple, draped in royal blue, the avatar of progressivism, polished for mass consumption.

At stage right: Dean "The Glove" Banjo—World Series MVP turned freedom-first firebrand, Southern California businessman, and still the region's favorite son. His smile alone polled just above clean drinking water.

Between them stood two moderators with strained smiles and visibly clenched cue cards.

"Tonight's final gubernatorial debate," one began, "comes down to two candidates—one focused on progressive change and social equity, the other grounded in traditional values and economic reform."

Neither candidate flinched. Both had been media-trained to the point of automation.

Moderator One turned to Apple. "Mayor, let's start with you. California's economy is still recovering. Homelessness is on the rise. Why should voters believe your approach will bring lasting change?"

Apple smiled. "Because we have a plan rooted in what I call the 3E's: Empathy, Equity… and Electric Scooters."

Polite applause. Pixel exhaled backstage like she'd just cleared a TSA checkpoint.

Apple continued, "We are building a California that moves —not just on wheels, but in consciousness. A California that cares."

Dean grinned like a man waiting to hit a hanging curveball.

"Well, bless your heart, Mayor," he said. "That's a beautiful sentiment. I don't come with acronyms. I come with results. Championships. Leadership. Payroll discipline."

Louder applause. Camera three cut to a woman in a Banjo jersey, tearing up behind a foam finger.

Dean leaned in. "I know what it takes to win. Whether it's the bottom of the ninth or a budget shortfall—you need someone who doesn't flinch under pressure."

Moderator Two interjected, "What would you cut first in the budget, Mr. Banjo?"

Dean smiled again, broader this time. "First thing? Bureaucracy. Second thing? Excuses."

Moderator One turned back to Apple. "Mayor, response?"

Apple kept her smile. "Dean, you're good with soundbites. I'll give you that. But you said it yourself last month—'California needs to get back to its roots. To its past.'"

She turned slightly, looking directly at the camera.

"And that's exactly what you are, Dean. The past. A ballplayer from America's pastime trying to govern a state that's already sprinting toward the future."

The room paused. Then murmured. Then applauded—harder.

Pixel grinned backstage. News producers across the state clipped the moment, and social media influencers were already adding music to the bite.

Apple stood firm, surrounded afterward by cameras, Gail by her side, Javier just behind, waving and clapping like he'd just seen his cousins evade ICE agents.

"We are the future of California," Apple declared into the press scrum. "Inclusive, sustainable, forward-facing. And unafraid of change."

Somewhere on the far end of the arena, behind the sound rig and a half-dozen interns with ring lights, Frank and Ron stood against a railing. Frank wore a faded T-shirt that read `Firefighters Do It With Water` and a Dodgers cap pulled low, the kind of outfit that made him look more like a heckler on beer break than a man once trusted with a city's emergencies.

Ron sipped from a complimentary espresso shot. "She really said it. Called him 'the past.' That's cold."

Frank nodded, quiet.

"Still thinking about Orange County?" Ron asked.

Frank didn't respond right away. He just watched the political circus unfold—handlers and press circling the mayor like lemmings, ready to follow her off a cliff, same as the rest of California.

"I'm just wondering," he said, "how many people here actually believe any of this."

Ron smirked, raising his cup.

"Same folks who think profile pics are real and campaign promises come with warranties. Gullibility's bipartisan."

Frank chuckled at Ron's line, a dry, tired laugh that cut through the noise around them.

But then it hit him.

His smile faded as the reality sank in—Orange County wasn't just a new post. It was distance. Finality. The quiet admission that whatever thread still tethered him to Gail... was fraying fast.

"What about Gail? This is probably the final nail," he said quietly.

Ron looked over.

"If I take the job down there," Frank said, eyes still on the stage, "that's it. That's the end of it—with Gail."

Ron gave a small shrug. "Yeah. Probably."

He handed Frank the rest of his espresso. "But at least now you know where you stand. Which is more than most people get—in politics or marriage."

Frank stared at Gail one more time, then turned away.

And somewhere, in all the excitement, Northern California was over—its promise folding shut not with hope, but with the flimsy flutter of a campaign pamphlet drifting in the wind.

CHAPTER 27
AND THE WINNER IS...

"What Orwell feared were those who would ban books. What Huxley feared was that there would be no reason to ban a book, for there would be no one who wanted to read one."

— **NEIL POSTMAN,**
AMUSING OURSELVES TO DEATH

The kiss of the rising sun lit up the dashboard of the first-generation Prius, ushering to life the majestic Golden Gate Bridge. Below the iconic span, the wind whipped the bay waters into a white-capped fury.

For Frank Wright, a deep, cleansing breath now felt closer to static than clarity—just noise between the

signals. Election Day arrived with the pageantry of a parade and the sincerity of a talent show.

Fire Station 11—Frank's Fire Station 11, once home to soot-stained gear and half-eaten granola bars—now buzzed with political handlers, local influencers, and journalists in smart-casual desperation. The fire pole had been cordoned off with velvet rope. Someone had wheeled in a kombucha bar. A drone hovered overhead for a livestream called *Democracy After Dark.*

Mayor Apple stood at the center of the chaos, commanding attention in a sharply tailored pantsuit and a smile so white it made camera lenses flinch. She shook hands with the polish of a seasoned politician and waved with the poise of royalty on a farewell tour—confident, curated, and completely in control.

Javier stood at her side, the perfect state-issued puppet, grinning the gospel of DEI and practically wrapped in a Honduran flag. Behind them, Jax and the rest of Apple's 3E coalition arranged themselves with glossy precision—smiles rehearsed, roles assigned, every demographic box accounted for.

Pixel worked the room as if wired into the circuitry—cross-referencing spreadsheets, coordinating interviews, and pretending not to panic. Gail sat near the engine bay doors, watching it all unfold with the detached air of someone attending her own coming-out party without a cake.

The mayor had told her she'd be going to Sacramento. Head of Diversity for the 3E Initiative. Big job. Big salary. But with Apple, promises were campaign slogans—easy to say, harder to cash in.

She glanced at the stage.

A temporary platform stood against the fading sky, the sun sinking but not yet gone. Apple glowed under the ring lights, framed by rising cheers and the restless flicker of cameras.

Gail's mind drifted to Frank.

To Orange County.

To the sudden stillness of what their marriage had become.

She hadn't told anyone—not even Pixel—but she'd thought about going with him. Starting over. Living outside the bubble of optics and messaging. No panels. No press. Just a clean start.

But then the crowd erupted.

Pixel came sprinting across the room, waving her phone like it was the Holy Grail.

"We won!"

A news alert blinked across every screen in the station:

DEAN 'THE GLOVE' BANJO CONCEDES.
APPLE ELECTED GOVERNOR IN HISTORIC
LANDSLIDE.

Apple didn't celebrate. She absorbed it—standing taller, smiling wider, already speaking with her eyes to a higher office. Her ascension had always felt inevitable. Now it was fact.

She turned and walked directly to Gail.

"Pack your bags," she said, voice low and certain. "You're coming to Sacramento. You're my new Director of Diversity. It's official."

Gail blinked. "You're serious?"

Apple nodded. "You'll help me build the California of tomorrow."

Pixel materialized like a genie with a clipboard. "We're also spinning up an NGO alongside the department. A civic arm of the 3E movement. Workshops, scooters, public empathy campaigns. We'll get you a logo by Monday."

Gail hesitated. "NGO?"

Pixel laughed, "Non-Government Organization."

"Oh, alright. And the funding?"

"Oh, it's solid," Pixel said with the kind of grin that came from knowing the deck was stacked. "State-backed, privately managed. We'll have a board—some friendly faces.

Think: innovation through influence. And more importantly, permanence. The NGO builds an apparatus that doesn't just run programs—it sends money back to the party, secures campaign continuity, and keeps the machinery humming well past one election cycle. This isn't just about surviving a budget fight, Gail. This is Sacramento locked down. One term, two terms, maybe more."

Gail half-knew there was more beneath the promise, but she refused to entertain it—not now, not in this moment of victory. After eighteen years of silence, here was a taste of something alive, something hers. Stanford had been the dream she abandoned; Sacramento could be the stage where she finally stepped into her own light. The apple might be forbidden, but right now it was sweet, and she was hungry.

Pixel leaned closer, voice lowering. "And with you at the front of it all, you're not just helping the governor blaze a trail. You're setting the path for something higher. Washington higher."

It was all too surreal for Gail, as if she'd slipped into someone else's script. She glanced toward the glass doors—through them, she could see both lives at once: the old one with Frank, worn but real, and the new one in government, polished and uncertain. She loved Frank, always would, but in her mind, he represented the past—just as the mayor had said. The other door stood waiting, not with power for its own sake, but with the chance to reclaim the woman she had once set out to be.

Outside, the last light of day stretched thin across the bay, a final brushstroke of gold giving way to violet.

Then the fire alarm sounded, a shrill reminder of what the building was meant to be. No one moved. The crew was too busy raising glasses, spilling champagne over turnout coats that hadn't seen a fire in months. Victory drowned out duty, and the siren wailed on, ignored.

Frank was halfway through a shift when his phone lit up.

Incoming Call: RON

He sighed, tapped the screen, and kept one hand on the wheel.

"Apple won," Ron said—no hello. "Banjo struck out before he even left the on-deck circle. The news calls it a 'generational mandate.' Pixel's crying on livestream, Javier's saluting with a mango, and Gail—well, the cameras can't get enough of her."

Frank stared at the red light ahead.

"You still there?"

"Yeah," Frank said. "I'm here."

"You don't sound thrilled."

"I've been numb for months. Hard to cheer for the circus when you've already ridden in the clown car."

"Well," Ron said, "at least your clown car doesn't have to say Uber on the side anymore."

Frank gave a half-smile—right as a new ride request buzzed through.

Pickup: Fisherman's Wharf

"Gotta go," he said. "Duty calls."

He hung up and turned toward the waterfront.

Five minutes later, he pulled up near a chain crab shack as tourists snapped selfies with chowder. A woman stood under a vintage sign.

He knew her instantly—even with the platinum wig and oversized sunglasses.

Sheila. Or as she once called herself, Aleihs—her personal brand of mischief.

She waved like they were old friends.

Frank didn't slow down. He coasted past her, turned right on a one-way, and never looked back.

He felt something close to relief.

Let the Bay Area keep its chaos. He was heading south—to a firehouse without cameras, a town without character back-stories, and a life that didn't include women with reversible names.

He rolled down the window, breathed in the salty evening air, and hit *Go Offline* on the rideshare app.

Then his phone buzzed again.

Frank stared at the screen.

NEW MESSAGE: STEFANIA

He hesitated, thumb hovering.

Part of him wanted to ignore it—chalk it up to timing, regret, whatever version of closure people chased when they ran out of better options.

But curiosity had a way of surviving even when everything else was tired.

He tapped it open.

STEFANIA: Hey. I don't know if you're still in the city… but I saw your name pop up on the app. Weird, right?

Anyway… if you're around, maybe we could talk. No pressure. I'm at Dolores Park for a bit. Just sitting. A few people around. It's a nice evening.

He read it again. Slowly.

No emoji. No performance. No sharp edges.

Just her.

He sat in the quiet, dashboard lights washing over him in soft blue.

Then he shifted into drive. And turned toward the park.

Dolores Park was unusually still. A few scattered couples lounged on blankets, their murmurs low and intimate. Off in the distance, a group of friends passed around a joint, laughter rising and fading like a breeze. Dog walkers shuffled past under the glow of old streetlamps, leashes loose, voices carrying low across the sidewalk.

The breeze moved easy, carrying the sharp hint of eucalyptus and the warm drift of someone's takeout—Thai, maybe.

Frank spotted her near the crest of the hill, sitting cross-legged on a blanket, nursing a thermos and watching the city below.

She turned as he approached. "You made good time."

"You picked the one hill in San Francisco I still know how to find," Frank said, settling in beside her.

They sat in silence, watching the lights flicker.

"I caught the mayor's speech," she said. "They did it from Fire Station 11."

Frank didn't answer.

Stefania glanced over. "That's where you used to work, right?"

He nodded. "Used to, yeah."

She took a sip from the thermos, then set it down beside her knee. "I saw Javier. The whole cast. And I realized something... You were the one they replaced."

Frank turned toward her.

"You were the placeholder. The sacrifice for the 3E rollout. Empathy, Equity... and whatever else fit on a bumper sticker."

"Electric scooters," Frank muttered.

She smiled, but it faded quickly. "They sold a narrative. You didn't fit the look, so they wrote you out."

Frank exhaled. "It's politics. I was naïve enough to think I mattered—that merit mattered."

"You did," she said. "You just didn't photograph well under the Apple filter."

That made him laugh. Not bitter—just tired.

"I should've told you more," he said after a moment. "About Gail. About the job. About… all of it."

"I figured most of it out," Stefania said, pulling her knees in. "Still, would've been nice to hear it from you."

Frank nodded. "I guess I wanted a few licks at the lollipop before I got to the chewy truth."

She gave a small laugh. "I get it. I put Portugal as my 'spiritual home' on my profile. Truth is, I got dumped there after a wine tour. But 'spiritual home' gets more licks."

They laughed, not as strangers now.

Then silence, warm and intact.

Stefania looked out at the skyline. "Maybe the better stories don't start with chemistry or bios. Maybe they start simple. No expectations. No apps. Just… people. Friends first."

Frank looked at her. Really looked at her. Not through the lens of what might be or could've been, but as someone who, against odds, still sat beside him after everything.

"Friends first," he repeated. "That'd be a refreshing change."

"I'm not saying you're off probation," she said. "But I'd share a park bench with you again."

He smiled. "I'm heading to Orange County. Got a post at a station down there. Close to Disneyland. Feels like a second shot."

"Oh, ok. That's good," she said. "You need that."

They sat a moment longer. Down the hill, a skateboard ticked over cracked pavement. Just beyond the trees, a patrol car idled in quiet watch. She'd chosen this park for a reason—it was one of the few places in the city that still felt safe after dark.

"If your compass ever swings south," Frank said, rising, "well… maybe that's fate's way..."

Stefania interrupted him. “I’ve followed worse signs.”

They both smiled.

He gave a small wave and turned toward his car.

He didn’t look back.

She didn’t expect him to.

CHAPTER 28

WELCOME TO THE HOTEL CALIFORNIA

"You can check out any time you like, but you can never leave."

— **EAGLES**, *HOTEL CALIFORNIA*

The kiss of the rising sun lit up the tinted windows of the Capitol Annex, ushering to life a Sacramento skyline still draped in ambition and early traffic. Outside her office, the palms swayed—a borrowed beauty in a city built on managed growth.

In the glass reflection of her office window, Gail saw the outline of a woman she no longer was—her old life lingering like a silhouette, familiar but finished.

Gail's new office smelled like the start of a play—fresh paint, stiff curtains, and the faint tension of a script everyone had agreed to follow but no one had fully read.

A framed print of the 3E logo—`Empathy. Equity. Electric Scooters`—hung slightly crooked above her state-issued desk. Next to it, a freshly mounted emblem for Digital Public Infrastructure's *50in5* initiative—five cartoon continents stitched together by giant QR codes, ringed with the slogan "Half a Decade, Half the Globe, All Your Data"—beamed like a motivational poster from a future no one asked for.

Gail caught herself staring at it, wondering if this was what progress looked like now: a branding exercise with better clip art.

Pixel buzzed around, still riding the afterglow of the election. "We'll get you a standing desk," she said. "And maybe one of those Himalayan salt lamps. Optics love wellness." Gail smiled politely and turned toward the Capitol dome outside her window.

Pixel stood near the window, scanning her tablet and casually assessing the room. "Not bad. Neutral tones, decent light. You'll look credible in every direction."

Above a nearby bookshelf, TC the cat was curled like a furry question mark, yawning as if unimpressed by government appointments. His eyes tracked the room lazily, clearly hoping something small would move.

Gail glanced up. "He's still adjusting."

Pixel smirked. "Aren't we all."

Gail gave a faint smile, smoothing the front of her blazer. She hadn't worn one this stiff since her days at Stanford—twenty-one years ago, studying environmental engineering and believing she'd change the world from the inside out. That was before Frank. Before the firehouse. Before her ideals got repackaged into… marriage.

Now here she was—Director of 3E Initiatives for the Governor of California.

A knock, then a sudden flurry.

The door burst open, and in swept Governor Apple—followed by two cameras, a campaign documentarian, and a guy with a boom mic wearing cowboy boots, mirrored sunglasses, and a smug grin that didn't belong in government buildings.

"This is where the real work begins!" Apple announced. "Everyone, meet Gail Wright. Kansas roots, San Francisco grit, and now Sacramento vision. She's going to be the heartbeat of 3E."

Gail managed a nod, but her eyes locked on the boom mic bobbing overhead. It trembled slightly, not from movement—but from barely contained amusement.

She squinted. The boots were too familiar. The gum, too loud. The smirk... unmistakable.

The boom mic dipped a little too low.

"Ron?" she mouthed.

He grinned and gave a subtle cowboy-boot shuffle, mouthing back, *"Union gig. Dental included."*

Gail blinked once, hard—like that might reset the simulation.

Governor Apple clapped her hands. "Okay, team, let's get some B-roll of 'thoughtful collaboration.' Pixel, find a flattering filter. We want authenticity, but, you know... not too authentic."

The cameras rolled. Apple smiled wide enough to be legally binding.

Then, just as quickly, she turned and was gone—already onto her next soundbite, probably in another building.

Pixel leaned against the door, "She calls that governing by drive-by. It's her thing."

Gail sat back in her chair, trying to adjust to a reality that felt not unlike a very expensive hallucination. "I'm in charge now?"

"Until we blame you for something," Pixel grinned. "So, probably a good six months."

She reached into her tote bag and pulled out her phone. "Speaking of being in charge… You ready to date again?"

Gail groaned. "Pixel…"

"I'm just saying. New title. New city. New algorithm."

Gail laughed. "I'm currently on the No Man diet. High in boundaries, low in drama."

Pixel smirked. "That's cute. Sadly, there's no 'celibate but curious' filter."

She tapped her screen. "You're doing this, Gail. You're the most eligible Director of Equity in the state—and this app? Small pool, high standards."

She turned the phone toward her, already swiping. "You're about to be single, visible, and surrounded by men in a city who quote Rousseau and think watching women's beach volleyball counts as feminist solidarity. Trust me—you need this."

LibLaughLove.com

"Where shared beliefs lead to better relationships."

Gail raised an eyebrow. "That's a real tagline?"

"They beta tested it on a TED Talk audience," Pixel said flatly. "It matches you based on values, voting record, and whether they own hiking boots but get winded using stairs." She laughed.

Gail squinted at the screen. "Is that guy... holding a compost bin?"

📍Logan, 42
Public Policy Consultant | Sacramento, CA
6'0"
Political Affiliation: Left of Center, but right of Burning Man
🚭 Non-smoker | 🍷 Rarely drinks | 🚸❌ No kids
Bio:
Recovering campaign manager. Still in love with public radio. Once fasted for climate justice (but cheated with kombucha). Looking for someone who understands both root vegetables and root causes.
Fun fact: My compost is more organized than my dating life.

Pixel nodded. "That's Logan. We've been texting. He says he's 'vegan-light' and open to poly, but only on weekends. Look at his last photo… he's crying because *Ninja Turtles* got pulled from streaming. Says he can project empathy."

Gail swiped. Another profile popped up.

📍Warren, 39
Freelance Researcher / Professional Panelist
Political Affiliation: Democratic Socialist with capitalist impulses
🍷 Drinks socially | 🌿 420 friendly |
🚸❌ No kids

Bio:
I'm not saying I wrote a white paper on intimacy in post-capitalist structures, but I'm also not *not* saying that. I own too many linen shirts and one rescue dog named Bernie.
Looking for:
Someone who knows their attachment style, their voting district, and how to parallel park under pressure. Someone to Feel the Bern with.

"Look, Gail," Pixel said, still swiping, "the Sacramento scene is about 80% earnest guys who peaked during intramurals. Half of them are holding Little League participation trophies in their pics like they're Congressional Medals of Honor."

Gail laughed, shaking her head. "Is this a dating app or a nostalgia museum?"

"Bit of both," Pixel said. "They're emotionally fluent, just... directionally challenged."

Gail frowned at one profile. "He listed 'feminism' under hobbies."

"Yeah, there's a lot of that. Also, guys with podcast mics and crypto regrets calling themselves 'visionaries in transition.'" Gail sighed. "Nope, been there, done that!"

Pixel smirked. "Come on, you hold the cards now, you're not dependent on a guy anymore—"

Gail nodded. "This is a landfill."

"No, it's a museum of soft boys with strong opinions. But listen—somewhere in that mess is a guy who'll actually text back and knows the difference between DEI and DUI."

Gail handed the phone back, still smiling. "I haven't dated since Bush was in office."

Pixel smirked. "Neither have most of them. The closest they've come to intimacy is shock and awe on a Friday night."

Gail paused. "I don't know, Pixel. It's all a little much."

Pixel lowered her voice. "Hey. When the revolution stalls, you might as well swipe through what's left of it."

And just then, the door creaked open.

She looked up.

Frank stood in the doorway.

His hair was a little longer, his eyes carrying the kind of tired that doesn't sleep off.

He was dressed as someone passing through—because that's exactly what he was.

"Knock, knock. I took a detour," he said gently, holding up a manila envelope. "Didn't want to drop these in the mail."

Gail stood. Her throat tightened, but she nodded. "Of course."

Pixel smiled at Frank and exited the office.

The Wrights moved to the desk like two diplomats at a quiet treaty signing.

No drama. Just pen, paper, and something else unspoken.

Frank looked around the office. "It suits you."

Gail smiled, letting her eyes sweep over the crooked logos and stiff curtains. "Yeah. Feels like it's been waiting."

He hesitated. "You'll do great here. I mean that."

She nodded. "And you'll do great down there. Orange County needs you."

A silence settled. Not heavy—just familiar. The kind that had texture but no sharp edges.

Frank cleared his throat. "What about Javi?"

Gail's smile flickered. "He's back in San Francisco—learning to put out fires without burning his fingers."

She reached for the envelope, then paused. "Oh, you just missed Ron."

Frank smiled. "Yeah, he's got a new gig—something semi-legit. He's working sound for the governor's media team. Says it's 'freelance civic engagement with boots on.' Still pitching his dating Cyrano on the side, though."

Gail raised an eyebrow. "Right, you mentioned it over the phone."

Frank nodded. "Apparently, Ron met some tech billionaire

in a float tank. The guy offered to 'advise,' and Ron heard that as a done deal."

Gail laughed. "Of course he did." She opened the envelope, glanced at the papers inside, and set them on the desk—divorce papers, crisp and unsigned until now.

They hugged—polite, warm, brief. When he pulled away, she didn't follow him with her eyes. She'd already done that too many times before.

After Frank left, Pixel came back to check on Gail.

"You okay?"

Gail exhaled slowly. "Yeah. I think I actually am."

She picked up her phone from the desk, tapped the screen, and started downloading the app.

Pixel grinned. "Look out, California. Gail 2.0 is coming."

Gail smiled, eyes still on the screen. "Not 2.0. Just me. Finally."

Outside, the California sun hit the dome just right.

And inside, something new began.

About the Author

Joel D. Bradley is a former international baseball scout with Major League Baseball and holds a degree in Creative Writing from the University of Miami. He is the author of two non-fiction books, Death By Data: How Analytics and Technology Are Killing Baseball and The Seven-Player Baseball Revolution.

Bradley splits his time between Waxahachie, Texas, and Fort Lauderdale, Florida. He has two grown sons and two granddaughters. In addition to his writing, he is available for select speaking engagements.

For inquiries, please contact him at:

joel@elliscountybooks.com

Also by Joel D. Bradley

- The Seven-Player Baseball Revolution
- Death By Data: How Analytics and Technology Are Killing Baseball

ELLIS COUNTY BOOKS

An independent publisher based in Waxahachie, Texas

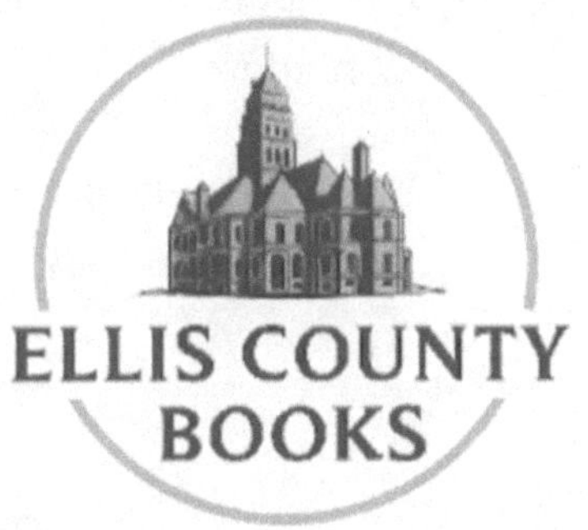

NOTES TO READERS

If you enjoyed Swipe Wright, please consider leaving a review online.
Your feedback helps independent authors reach new readers.

www.ingramcontent.com/pod-product-compliance
Lightning Source LLC
LaVergne TN
LVHW100517110826
845146LV00002B/673

* 9 7 9 8 9 9 3 3 6 5 1 0 7 *